HIRAM'S FAITH

HIRAM'S FAITH

BLAKE HABER

BLACK LANTERN PRESS
SANTA BARBARA

Published by Black Lantern Press
Santa Barbara, California
www.blakehaber.com

Book design: Blake Haber
Front cover Art: Mark Thomas
Rear cover illustration based on "A mosquito (*Aedes aegypti*)" by A.J.E. Terzi, courtesy of the Wellcome Collection. Original work has been cropped and edited for this design. Licensed under CC BY 4.0.

ISBN Paperback: 979-8-9940925-1-4

First Black Lantern Press Paperback Edition: April 2026

For Michelle

1

New York City, December 1851

BLOOD. BLACK BILE. YELLOW BILE. PHLEGM.

Professor Woodbridge slashed the words across the blackboard, then wheeled to face the packed auditorium.

"Gentlemen," he bellowed, "the essence of medicine lies in the balance of these four bodily humors. When they are in harmony, we have health, we have vigor. We have happiness. When they are not, we have sickness, we have feebleness. We have misery.

"But these conditions are not the mere symptoms of an imbalance. They are an insult to Man and to Nature, a corruption demanding correction. And who shall correct it? We shall. Not with wishful thinking, not with superstition, and most assuredly not with prayer. We shall do it with science, with real medicine, grounded in reason, revealed through observation, and proven by rigorous application."

Woodbridge scanned the room, forehead glistening, eyes blazing, daring any of us to waver in our rapt attention. He spun to the blackboard.

"Take, for instance, the miraculous properties of—" he paused to chalk the words *mercurous chloride* across the slate. "Otherwise known as calomel, a purgative unmatched in its ability to rouse the liver, expel foul humors through the bowels, and cleanse the blood."

As Woodbridge lectured on, my gaze wandered to the windows lining the right side of the amphitheater-style lecture hall. Outside, snow fell steadily, blanketing Washington Square Park in white.

"Bloodletting!" Woodbridge thundered, underlining the word with another violent stroke. "A science perfected through the millennia. Any excess must be drawn off, whether by leech or by blade."

It was then, as I gazed across the snowy expanse, that I saw him for the first time: a lone figure standing among the trees.

"Without this vital therapy," Woodbridge intoned, "inflammation festers, the humors stagnate and putrefy; incapacitation and death swiftly follow."

At first, I wasn't sure whether it was a man at all, and not a tree trunk or a statue. But as I fixed my attention on the form, its outline sharpened, and I knew without a doubt that it was a man.

"Arsenic!" Woodbridge declared, sweeping his hand through the air as if casting a magic spell. "For the treatment of syphilis, ulcers, and malaria, it has no rival."

The man in the park wore a long black coat that flared at the hem and a comically tall top hat. He stood utterly still, save for the edges of his coat flapping in the wind. He might have been nothing more than a man taking shelter among the trees; yet even from this distance, something about him unsettled me deeply.

"Strychnine," Woodbridge went on. "In the hands of a skilled physician, it revitalizes the sluggish body, strengthens the heart and nerves, cures paralysis, exhaustion, and—most importantly—impotence."

The man stamped his feet in the snow, then turned.

I blinked. Was he looking at me?

"Whitaker!"

I flinched and tore my gaze from the window.

Woodbridge stood erect, hands on hips, elbows flared. "I said, would you care to enlighten us as to the exact dosage of strychnine, per the *United States Pharmacopeia*, for an adult female requiring nervous stimulation?"

"A thirtieth of a grain," I answered without needing to think.

"Correct," Woodbridge said, sweeping his gaze around the room. "Not that I'm surprised."

As he resumed his lecture, my eyes drifted back to the snowy landscape beyond the window.

But the man among the trees was gone.

I didn't believe in ghosts. But the way he had stood, still and unshaken as a gravestone in the wind, and the way he had seemed to stare at me through the glass, left a chill in me that would linger for hours.

I forced my attention back to the blackboard, where Professor Woodbridge was writing *LAUDANUM* in bold strokes.

"Opium in alcohol," he said, "offers mercy for even the gravest afflictions. For cholera, coughing, and—most helpfully—sleepless infants, laudanum is a boon to the patient and to the medical profession alike."

And so he carried on, theatrically demanding our attention. But I couldn't give him mine; the image of the figure in the snow had fixed itself behind my eyes, dimming every other thought to shadow.

The following Monday, as I studied the exam grades on the notice board in the hall, Professor Woodbridge approached.

"Good show, Whitaker."

"Sir?"

"Only perfect score in the College of Medicine. You should be proud."

"Oh. Yes, sir. Thank you."

"Tell me, what are your plans for after graduation?"

"Plans? Oh, I've been thinking about going to California."

His brow furrowed. "California? What in the—with your talents? Forget that wasteland. Stay here. Join the faculty. Someone's got to take my place someday, don't they?"

"Thank you, sir. Yes, I'll think about it."

"Promise me you will. Think about it good and hard. And then do the smart thing and stay here in New York. Don't waste that gift of yours—" he tapped the side of my head—"on those know-nothing heathens out in California."

"I'll try not to, sir."

"Good show. Going to the Winter Social tomorrow?"

"No, sir. I'd like to get a head start on next semester's texts."

"Go to the Social. Life's short. Live a little."

He punched my shoulder lightly, winked, and strode off down the hall.

The waltz began. The men surged forward in crisp tailcoats and gleaming boots. The women, adorned in silk and satin, skirts billowing like storm clouds over layers of petticoats, swirled into the embrace of their partners.

I lingered by the wall, unpartnered, my eye on no one in particular, watching the dancers glide by. Before long, the air grew stifling. I turned to go.

But a face stopped me.

A young woman in a blue gown leaned against the far wall beneath the word *Winter* on the banner. I'd seen her before without paying much attention, but now something about her—her quiet poise and the way her dark curls cast swirly shadows across her lightly blushed cheeks—caught my eye.

On impulse, I crossed the room, weaving through the waltzing couples. When I reached her, I bowed.

"Good evening, miss," I said. "Allow me to introduce myself. Hiram T. Whitaker."

She extended a delicate hand gloved in white lace. I took it and brushed my lips lightly against it.

"A pleasure to meet you, Mr. Whitaker. Mary Beth Johansson, from Philadelphia."

"I believe I've seen you in the quad, Miss Johansson. Near the medical wing. I'm studying there, to be a physician."

"Oh, you're going to be a doctor? That's very impressive."

"And what about you?"

"I assist in the infirmary," she said, her warm smile catching the glow of a nearby candle as she waved to a girl waltzing past. "But I hope to become a nurse someday."

"That's very impressive, too," I said, raising my voice to be heard over the orchestra. "Perhaps you—"

But before I could finish, she'd slipped her arm through mine and led me onto the dance floor.

A few days later, Mary Beth and I sat together on a bench in the quad, bundled against the cold. Snow from the recent storm still blanketed the ground, and the maple trees, so recently ablaze with autumn color, stood bare.

"What do you intend to do when you graduate?" Mary Beth asked.

"Get away from here," I said. "As far as possible."

"Really? But why?" She looked around at the snowy landscape. "I find it rather lovely here in New York. Don't you?"

I glanced across the quad.

"Yes, but everything feels so... predetermined. One knows exactly what to expect, one day to the next. I'd prefer not to know what tomorrow might bring. Novelty quickens the blood, don't you think?"

"I suppose it must. And I do like the idea of it—travel, adventure."

We sat in silence for a while, watching our breath rise to form fleeting shapes in the frigid air.

"When you say far, do you mean London, or Paris?" she asked. "Or China? I've heard—"

"California."

"California? Do you mean you intend to dig for gold in those muddy camps?"

"Not at all," I said, turning to her. "The Chinese miners, the adventurers from all over the world, people with no knowledge of modern medicine, struggling to survive in a harsh and desperate land—imagine the opportunities for a man trained in medicine and the scientific method. Imagine the good he could do."

Embarrassed by my eager display of enthusiasm, I turned away.

A moment later, Mary Beth's mittened hand rested on mine.

"I imagine there would be opportunities for a nurse in California, too," she said.

2

February 1852

Mary Beth and I lay in my narrow bed reading letters from her parents. Her presence here in my room in men's student housing was strictly forbidden, but we didn't care. It was early evening, snowing outside, and so cold that the fire in the small fireplace did little to warm us. We pulled the meager covers tight, more for closeness than for warmth.

I picked up her father Gerry's letter to me and continued reading it aloud: "She wrote that she loves you and will marry you—despite your self-professed lack of faith—in a church or out in the street, it makes no difference to her. But I assure you, Hiram, it makes a world of difference to me and, more importantly, to Mary Beth's mother, who hasn't stopped crying since she read our daughter's letter announcing your intentions."

I looked over at Mary Beth. "Your poor mother."

"I'm sorry, Hiram. She's always been so dramatic."

I continued reading: "Our daughter is the most important thing in the world to us. And now she tells us she's going to California with you to make your fortune together.

To undertake such a difficult voyage with no guarantee of success is a dangerous notion. I pray you'll have the sense to reconsider. If not for yourself, then for our daughter.

"There are many opportunities for a man of your chosen profession here in Philadelphia. But if your mind is made up, then you must promise us you'll take good care of her and devote your life to her protection and well-being. If any harm should befall her, we could never recover from the loss, and could never forgive you for it."

"My parents should've run a theater, not a grocery store," Mary Beth said.

"Her mother and I should be happy," I read. "Our wild horse of a daughter is marrying a man who can tend to her when she stumbles and patch her up when she falls. And we are happy. We have discussed it at length and decided to give you our blessing.

"May God, too, bless both of you.

"Sincerely, Gerry Johansson."

I set down the letter and looked at Mary Beth.

"That's it, then," she said. "They've given us their blessing."

"Then let's get married."

"Let's!"

A clerk at City Hall directed us to a small room where a man in a rumpled coat sat behind a cluttered desk. He barely glanced up as we approached.

"Your names?" he asked.

"Hiram T. Whitaker."

"Mary Beth Johansson."

"Do you both enter this union freely?"

"We do," we replied in unison.

He stood and brushed a few crumbs from the front of his coat. "Then, by the authority vested in me by the City of New York, I declare you husband and wife. Sign here."

He pushed the ledger toward us. We took turns signing and dating it—February 13, 1852.

"Rings?" the magistrate prompted.

I found the silver ring in my pocket and slid it onto Mary Beth's finger. She regarded it for a moment, smiled, then slid a slim gold band onto mine.

"Congratulations," he said, snapping the book shut.

A few weeks later, I sat for my spring exams ahead of schedule, Mary Beth and I needing to catch the Mormon wagon train departing from Independence on April 9. I passed with respectable marks, collected my degree, and together we set off for Philadelphia, where I would meet Mary Beth's parents for the first time.

3

New Orleans, June 1853

I leaned against the damp, filthy window frame, my body shaking slightly, and looked out at the Mississippi River, a slate-colored smear in the distance, barely visible through the relentless downpour.

The previous month had baked the city dry—the *Picayune* newspaper had called it the driest May on record. Now the heavens appeared hell-bent on drowning New Orleans in a single day and washing all the detritus—human and otherwise—into the river.

I dressed painfully and descended the six flights to the street, where I took shelter beneath the cigar factory's awning. Smoking was a filthy habit, but I had to admit the aroma wafting from the door was pleasant enough. I peered in at the two men rolling cigars behind the counter. One glanced at me, smiled, and waved. I nodded, then turned away.

Dodging puddles and splashes from the filthy water rushing in the gutter along the banquette—as they called the wooden sidewalks here—I hurried up the street to the

Café du Petit Coin, where I bought a cup of coffee and a newspaper and settled into my usual seat by the window, facing St. Louis Street.

Just then, a dray passed by, piled high with small, unpainted coffins. In the heat and rain, a pale mist rose from them, giving the eerie impression of spirits escaping from within. I craned my neck as the wagon trundled past, watching it bump and sway up the rutted, partially flooded street.

Sitting back in my chair, I turned to the newspaper's editorial page, where the first column greeted me with an angry screed about the city's refusal to address the problem of the garbage rotting in the streets. The editor blamed the public's disdain for taxes, along with the council members' fear of losing their lucrative, do-nothing jobs. He then turned to the subject of mosquitoes, declaring them a nuisance but offering an unexpected note of optimism:

> As they ravage us with their incessant buzzing and biting, we can take solace in one undeniable truth: no God was ever so cruel as to afflict the same city with the twin scourges of mosquitoes and yellow fever. It can be taken as an act of faith that the summer of 1853 will go down in history as the healthiest one our fair city has ever been blessed to enjoy.

I smiled despite myself. As a man of science, I preferred not to rely on faith. Yet I found the sentiment oddly uplifting.

I skimmed a few more articles, mostly about the city council's infighting, before turning—almost as an afterthought—to the Notices and Obituaries page.

A Mr. Tobias Landry had lost a gold pocket watch, monogrammed "T.L.B.," on Royal Street. The St. Charles Cotillion Club would be hosting a ball on June 10th at the St. Charles Hotel Ballroom, formal attire required. The steamer *Magnolia* would be departing for Natchez and Vicksburg on June 3rd. A reliable individual was sought to assist in the collection of medicinal leeches—must be comfortable with brackish water and swamp travel. There would be a public whipping in Jackson Square at 8 a.m. on June 1st.

In the months since I'd arrived in New Orleans, I'd made a habit of avoiding whippings. If I heard talk of one, I left the room. If I saw a suspicious gathering in the distance, I turned down a different street. I'd nearly convinced myself they were a myth—a grotesque invention meant to cast the South in an unflattering light.

Perhaps it was the unrelenting rain soaking the city, or those child-sized caskets steaming in the heat. Or maybe it was the absence of morphine in my blood—I'd been trying to wean myself off it for weeks now with little success. Whatever the cause, I found myself suddenly afflicted with a morbid curiosity. I glanced at the clock on the café's wall.

A quarter to eight.

The newspaper fell from my hands.

I pushed back my chair, bolted out into the rain, and made my way down Levee Street to Jackson Square. There, a hundred or so people had already gathered beneath the Upper Pontalba Building's arcade, chatting happily despite the downpour—and the pending atrocity. I threaded my way through them until I reached a spot with an unobstructed view of the raised platform at the square's center.

There, tied to a post, stood a black man. He was shirtless, and his tattered britches, soaked through and sagging under the weight of the rain, clung to his legs. His arms were stretched upward, wrists bound tightly to the post with rope. His head was bowed, forehead resting against the wood. Rain pummeled his bare back.

Closer to the platform, clusters of onlookers stood beneath black umbrellas. Mostly police or slave owners, I guessed. At a distance, three black women huddled together beneath a single umbrella. Relatives of the man on the post, perhaps, or maybe just friends.

As I stared across the square at the man on the platform and the authorities surrounding him, a noise clanged inside me—a rough, metallic sound, like a rusty lever being thrown or a hatch forced open.

They can't possibly go through with this, I thought.

I scanned the crowd, searching for any sign that someone might rush forward and put a stop to this brutal spectacle before it began. But the throng buzzed with anticipation, and no one moved.

I had barely turned to face the platform when the whipmaster stepped forward, uncoiled his whip, and drew it back. Unable to watch, I looked down at my shoes instead. Seconds later, the crack of the whip split the air, and as if some invisible hand had grabbed my chin and yanked it upward, I looked up to see a fine red mist bloom above the platform. I gasped.

Around me, the onlookers roared their approval.

I shouldn't have come here. Bearing witness to this man's suffering was a useless gesture.

Yet I stood rooted to the spot, my eyes fixed on the man on the post. And as I stared in frozen horror, he turned his head and looked directly at me. I glanced left, then right, praying his gaze was meant for someone else. Anyone else. But there was no mistaking it: it was meant for me, and me alone.

I couldn't bear it. I looked away.

And as I did, I saw a familiar face in the crowd: that of J.W. McFarland, director of the Board of Health and, more importantly to me, head of the Medical Board, which oversaw the licensing of physicians and pharmacists in Louisiana.

Noticing me, he stepped forward.

"Damn pitiful, wouldn't you agree, Whicket?" he said.

"Whitaker," I replied. "And yes, Doctor McFarland, this is one of the most pitiful—"

"Gloomy enough weather without that damnable nigger forcing us into the storm to witness his comeuppance."

I recoiled at his words but said nothing; my future success demanded that I remain in McFarland's good graces.

Yet as he continued his tirade about the so-called injustices the man on the post had inflicted upon "us," I felt something wobble inside me—a complex yet rickety structure I'd built to hold myself together during my difficult time in New Orleans. With every heartless word McFarland spoke, another chunk of mortar crumbled and another brick dislodged.

The whip cracked again. The man cried out, and I wanted to cry out with him.

Then, as if fleeing the thing collapsing inside me and barely aware of what I was doing, I turned away from McFarland, broke free from the crowd, passed through the gate, and marched into the square's sucking slop, knowing only that I must help the man on the post, no matter the cost.

Rain soaked me as I slogged through the mud toward the platform's steps, where I found my path to the whipping post blocked by three large men, one of whom raised a hand in warning. When I refused to stop, they descended upon me, grabbed me roughly, and dragged me backward toward the square's edge, my heels gouging parallel tracks in the mud as I struggled to break free.

The whip cracked again. The man's head slumped against the post.

"Enough!" I yelled, struggling against the men's hold. "He's had enough!"

They hauled me through the gate and threw me to the ground, where my head struck the cobblestones and bounced. Pain flashed through my skull and hot blood seeped across my scalp.

Energized by rage, I scrambled to my feet.

The largest of the three pointed a finger at me and shook his head before they turned and strode back toward the platform.

"Someone put that Yankee up there with his nigger boyfriend!" someone jeered, and the crowd erupted in laughter.

I bent to brush chunks of mud from my coat and trousers. As I straightened, I noticed McFarland watching me. The chill in his gaze told me I should measure my next moves carefully. He was right: if I tried that stunt again, those men might really hurt me.

I gave a terse nod and turned toward the alley between the Cabildo—the old city hall—and St. Louis Cathedral.

"Excuse me, sir."

I halted near the Cabildo's arcade and turned to see a middle-aged woman in a Prussian blue dress standing beneath a red umbrella.

"I saw what you did," she said. "That was very brave of you."

I gave a slight nod. "Not at all."

"It was."

"I just can't understand how anyone could do such a thing to another human being."

She smiled faintly. "You're not from around here, are you, Mr.—?"

"Whitaker. Hiram T. Whitaker, from New York City."

"I'm from New York myself," she said, extending a hand gloved in violet lace. "A pleasure to meet you, Mr. Whitaker. Patience Dufilho."

We shook hands. The name sounded familiar, but I couldn't place it.

We stepped beneath the arcade as the rain fell harder. Fortunately, the loud downpour nearly drowned out the crack of the whip and the cheers that followed. Still, I winced each time.

"It warmed my heart, what you did," she said. "But it does rather make one wonder what brought you to New Orleans."

"A riverboat," I replied, attempting levity, if only to ease my inner turmoil.

She smiled and nodded.

"Beyond that," I added, "I'm not quite sure. I often ask myself the same thing."

"A good man, and one with a sense of humor. You're becoming more rare—and, dare I say it, more charming—by the minute, Mr. Whitaker."

"Thank you, Mrs. Dufilho. I suppose, really, I came for want of a job."

"Oh? What sort of a job?"

"Medical doctor."

She raised her eyebrows.

"I haven't gotten my license yet," I added. "But I will soon enough. I'm doing my internship at Saint Anne's, just up the road."

"Then I imagine you'll have your work cut out for you."

"Work, Mrs. Dufilho?"

"It's going to be a bad season, don't you think?"

"Bad season?"

"I'm sure you've noticed the yellow fever is going around."

"None more than usual," I said, glancing at another wagonload of caskets rolling by in the distance.

"That's wonderful to hear," she said. "If you can't trust a medical doctor to know what's going on, then who can you trust?"

"No one, I suppose."

"You know, I was just on my way to Antoine's for breakfast tea. If you'd care to join me, we could escape this dreadful weather and continue our chat in more civilized surroundings. I suspect we've much to talk about."

"I'd enjoy that very much, Mrs. Dufilho. But I'm afraid I have work to do. I'm already late. On account of..."

I nodded toward the square.

"Of course. Then if I'm ever in need of a good doctor, I'll know where to find you. Perhaps we'll meet again someday."

"I hope so, Mrs. Dufilho. Take care."

I tipped my hat and headed up the alley, keeping close to the wall to avoid the rain.

Despite the horrors of the morning—and the warm blood trickling down the nape of my neck—I felt oddly buoyant after our encounter, uplifted by Mrs. Dufilho's kind words and gentle, friendly demeanor. Yet I remained faintly troubled by my inability to place her name.

It really was foolish, I thought, what I'd attempted to do in Jackson Square. My mind must've been fogged by the absence of my morning dose. I couldn't afford another mistake like that. Getting my medical license and opening my own practice had to be my first priorities. After that, come what may.

As I crossed the street to Saint Anne's, I resolved to lie low until I'd gotten my license. To blend in, to be as unremarkable as a single boll in a vast sea of cotton.

4

Moments after I'd scrubbed the mud from my hands and tied on a clean linen apron for my rounds, Nurse Emma appeared in the doorway to my cramped hospital office.

"Room 2," she said. "Thaddeus Boone. Yellow fever symptoms."

I followed her into the room to find Mr. Boone lying atop his blanket, trembling, eyes shut tight, shirt and trousers soaked through with sweat.

"Open your eyes, Mr. Boone," I said.

"Hurts to," he rasped.

"I need to see them to diagnose your ailment. Nurse Emma says you're showing signs of yellow fever."

He opened his eyes to a squint, and I gently pried the left one fully open with my fingertips. No trace of jaundice, fortunately.

"Muscle ache in the lower back and knees," Nurse Emma said. "Vomited straight through the night."

"Any blood or black bile in his vomit?"

"No."

"Influenza, then. Castor oil and bleeding, at once."

"Yes, doctor," she said, though she didn't move.

"Is there something else?" I asked.

"We'd like a moment to pray, before he gets too weak."

"There's no time for that. We need to begin his treatment immediately."

"Before I get too—" Boone gurgled, cut short by a phlegm-filled cough. His trembling hand reached for Nurse Emma's.

I rubbed my brow and sighed. "Go on, then."

Nurse Emma took Boone's hand in hers.

"It'll only take a moment," she said, bowing her head. "Heavenly Father, we seek Your divine healing and strength. We ask for Your hand to be upon this man, to ease his suffering and restore his health. May Your love surround him and bring him comfort and peace."

I stepped out to check on another patient. When I returned, Nurse Emma and Mr. Boone were quietly waiting, and a look of peaceful contentment had alighted upon the man's face.

Later, in the hospital's dining room, Nurse Emma sat down across from me and unwrapped her usual sandwich, a thin slice of pork between two slices of baguette.

"This is a Catholic hospital," she said. "Saint Anne's. I'd think you'd realize that by now."

I nibbled on my own sandwich, bread and butter. "I do realize it. But illness requires action, not words. It requires treatment. It requires correction."

"Faith provides comfort and hope," she replied. "Giving someone those things is action. It is treatment."

"Comfort and hope built on superstition don't treat anything, not in the long run. They don't correct anything. Just the opposite."

"Science and faith aren't mutually exclusive, Doctor Whitaker. Many find comfort in both."

"I find more comfort in the truth."

She gave me a long look. "The truth is what one believes."

I sighed. We'd had this same argument too many times before.

"It isn't. It's what can be seen. What can be touched."

"What about the wind?"

"Jesus," I muttered, "not John Three again." I knew John 3:8—the verse likening the Holy Spirit to the wind, felt but not seen—all too well. "Fine. You and Saint John have won again."

She smiled faintly. "What about love?"

My heart skipped a beat. I took another bite of my sandwich, which now tasted more of paper than butter.

"What about it?" I replied.

"Can you see it? Can you touch it?"

Yes, I thought. *And no.*

5

The rains continued for several weeks more, flooding the streets with pestilent muck. The municipal dog poisoners —it was rabies season, and the city typically allotted more funds to poisoning dogs than to other public health measures—had mostly fled or died. Yet an endless stream of canine carcasses still floated by or lodged themselves against the iron balcony columns.

The newspapers finally conceded the obvious: New Orleans was in the grip of a yellow fever epidemic. In response, the authorities began igniting kegs of gunpowder in the streets, an attempt to purify the air of miasma, the noxious swamp vapors they believed spread the fever. Some days, it was hard to tell whether I'd suffocate first from sulfurous smoke or drown in the relentless, Biblical rain.

I now took my morning coffee in the front room of the cigar factory below my apartment, as all the cafés had shut down, whether for lack of living patrons, workers, or both. Yet the cigar rollers carried on, seemingly unaffected by the disaster taking place beyond the windows. I'd never smoked before, but it seemed polite to sample the factory's wares if I was going to occupy one of their tables every day. The habit grew on me, and soon I couldn't imagine my mornings without a cigar, a cup of coffee, and a newspaper. One had to accept what joys life offered in times like these.

One morning, as I was lighting my cigar, I thought back to the first logjam of dead dogs I'd seen, lodged in the gutter out front. At the time, it had seemed like a strange and sinister omen. Now, such sights were mundane. It was the human bodies, strewn like garbage in the streets, that still unsettled me.

After several days, the authorities gave up on gunpowder and turned instead to barrels of burning tar. This newly "purified" air was more suffocating than ever, so they began firing cannons into the sky at regular intervals, hoping to punch holes through the smoke-choked atmosphere to let the miasma escape. Yet from all evidence at the hospital, reports from others, and the grim scenes in the streets, it was clear none of this had done a thing to quell the fever.

I put the paper down and let the calming sound of the cigar roller's knife tapping against the board transport me. After a moment, he began whistling a lilting tune. He'd whistled it before, and I'd always found it pleasant.

"Pedro," I said, "that's a lovely tune. May I ask what—"

Before I could finish, a bolt of lightning struck the middle of the river with a blinding flash. The thunderclap followed instantly, rattling the factory windows so violently that I leapt from my chair. As I did, I caught sight of two figures in the street: a woman tugging along a little girl, both pummeled by the relentless rain.

I grabbed my umbrella and dashed outside.

"Ma'am," I called, "take my umbrella!"

They stopped and turned, and for a moment, I froze, for the girl bore an uncanny resemblance to my sister Heather.

Regaining my senses, I ran to them and pressed the umbrella into the woman's hands, all the while unable to take my eyes off the child. The woman nodded her thanks and led her daughter away through the rain. I stood motionless, watching them fade into the storm, wondering whether I had only imagined the resemblance. After a moment, I returned to the cigar factory, picked up my cigar, and took a long puff.

"*Todo bien, Señor Whitaker?*" Pedro called from behind the counter.

"*Sí, Pedro, muy bien,*" I replied, forcing a smile.

He smiled in return, nodded, and went back to his rhythmic, methodical work.

I leaned back, closed my eyes, and let the thick, sweet smoke wash over me, imagining myself sitting on some distant shore, in a place untouched by memory or loss. But it wasn't enough to hold back the wave of grief the little girl's face had stirred.

Soon, it crashed over me.

Most of our patients at Saint Anne's were poor, hard-working people who lived and toiled in the surrounding streets. But occasionally, someone from the upper echelons of society came through our doors. James Beauregard, a cabinetmaker of some repute who resided in an opulent townhouse nearby, was one such man. He had arrived the previous day, neatly dressed and impeccably groomed, but for the bits of sawdust and dried black vomit mingling in his beard. His wife, Odette, had said he went to church twice a week and wasn't the sort of man God would just cast aside.

Yet here he lay, lifeless, despite my best efforts and Nurse Emma's most fervent prayers.

I set down my stethoscope. "If God could've saved him when you asked, then why didn't He?" I said to Nurse Emma. My frustration was aimed both at her prayers and the looming burden of having to inform Mrs. Beauregard of her husband's passing. "Why didn't He intervene in the first place, without needing to be begged to do it? What, precisely, did Mr. Beauregard do that so upset your precious God?"

"Hiram, please stop."

She had never called me by my first name before, and it caught me off guard.

"I'm sorry," I said.

"Do you think I don't ask myself the same thing? But that's the meaning of faith, isn't it? Only God knows why He does what He does. Everything happens for a reason. I have to believe that. Otherwise..." She paused and pulled the bile-soaked sheet over Mr. Beauregard's face.

"But what if there *isn't* a reason for everything?" I said. "What if Mr. Beauregard died for no reason at all? What then?"

"I can't even consider it."

I knocked on the front door of the Beauregard residence. It opened to reveal a plump black woman in a red-and-white dress peering out at me.

"Yes, sir?"

"Good afternoon, miss. I'm Doctor Whitaker, Mr. Beauregard's physician."

"That right?"

"I've come to speak with Mrs. Beauregard. About an unfortunate matter."

She hesitated.

"May I come in?" I asked.

"I believe Mrs. Beauregard passed."

"Passed?"

"Away."

My surprise and sorrow at hearing those two simple words—passed, away—were softened by an undeniable relief: I wouldn't have to deliver the news of Mr. Beauregard's death to his wife after all.

"Away?" I said, just to be certain.

"Yes, sir. Children too."

The woman and her daughter to whom I'd given my umbrella outside the cigar factory arrived at Saint Anne's a few days later, both feverish and coughing. I tended to them the moment they were settled in their beds.

"Evangeline and Antoinette Moreau," Nurse Emma said, nodding first toward the woman, then toward the girl.

"So you're a doctor," Evangeline murmured before falling back into her pillow with a damp thud.

"That's right, Mrs. Moreau."

I took her wrist to count her pulse, but lost track, distracted as I was by the girl's uncanny resemblance to my sister.

"I'll bring you your umbrella now that I know where to find you," Evangeline said, before breaking into a coughing fit.

"Keep it, Mrs. Moreau. You might need it for some time."

I checked her pulse again: slow and weak. Her forehead blazed beneath my hand. Her symptoms indicated surging yellow bile.

"Bleeding and castor oil," I told Nurse Emma.

She nodded and slipped out.

I turned my attention to Antoinette. Her pulse was sturdier than her mother's, but her forehead burned even hotter.

"Have you spat up any blood or black bile?" I asked.

"No," she whispered.

"That's good. You're going to be okay, Antoinette. You and your mother are in the best possible care here at Saint Anne's. I promise you."

I laid my hand on hers and gave it a gentle pat. An ache rose in my throat, and I let my hand rest there a moment longer than I'd intended.

The next morning, I arrived early to learn that Evangeline had recovered fully. She'd left for work, promising to return for her daughter by day's end. But Antoinette's condition had worsened. Her fever had spiked to 104, her vomit had turned yellow-green, her pulse was weaker, and her breathing shallower.

Given her fragile state, I forwent the scarifier—an eight-bladed tool used for urgent bloodletting—and used leeches instead, two on each leg.

Nurse Emma appeared in the dining room at lunchtime.

"A group of us are heading to the field hospital in Chalmette," she said. "They're overwhelmed by the fever and asked for help. We'll be back in two days. Can you join us?"

"I can't," I replied. "There are patients here who need me."

"Nurse Rebecca will be here. And there's a doctor from Charity Hospital filling in."

"I'm sorry, I can't."

"It's the little girl in Room 3, isn't it? Antoinette? I saw how you looked at her, how tenderly you treated her."

I nodded, my face growing hot. How sensitive Nurse Emma could be to the feelings of others.

"Nurse Rebecca—" she began again.

"I want to help, really. But I can't."

She studied me for a moment, then turned and walked away. I looked down at my untouched lunch.

Antoinette's mother didn't return that day. Worried about the girl, I stayed at the hospital and spent the night on a thin mat on my office floor. At dawn, I went to check on her.

She lay motionless. Her dress was soaked through and clinging to her delicate, bony hips. Her feet splayed at odd angles. Her chestnut hair, damp with sweat, was plastered to her scalp. Her eyes stared blankly at the ceiling.

For a terrible moment, I thought she was gone. A sharp pain bloomed in my chest, and I grabbed the bedpost to steady myself. But then she turned her head toward me, and the wave of relief washing over me was stronger than any dose of morphine.

"I dreamt about you, Doctor Whitaker," she said, her voice faint but clear.

"You did?"

"Yes. We were in a field of wildflowers together. You were on your knees, digging a hole with your bare hands. A tall man with a big hat stood next to you, holding a beautiful bouquet. I believe he must have picked the flowers himself."

A shiver ran through me. "A hole? What sort of hole?"

"I think it was a grave."

I pulled up a chair and sat beside her.

"Dreams don't mean anything, you know," I said. "They're just..."

Her eyes met mine. "Don't they, though?"

"Not at all."

"A fortune teller once told me they reveal the future."

"It isn't true," I said, swatting at a mosquito buzzing around my head. "If anything, they reveal the past."

"It might not have been a grave, anyway," she said.

"That's right."

The mosquito landed on my neck and I slapped at it, smearing its blood on my skin.

"But I wonder," I said, "do you have any idea whose grave it was?"

"Yours or mine," she replied, her gaze shifting back to the ceiling. "I'm uncertain which."

I forced a smile. "Neither of ours, I'm sure. But what about the tall man with the bouquet? Was he anyone you know?"

"I believe he was Baron Sunday."

"Baron—"

Before I could finish, her mother appeared in the doorway, soaked from the rain. She rushed to Antoinette's side and enveloped her in a tight embrace.

"Oh my God, baby, you're alive," she cried.

Tears streamed down her cheeks as she explained she'd been kept late in the American Quarter, caring for Mr. Calhoun's mother and children. The storm had made travel impossible, so she'd slept in their guest room and left at first light—without taking the time to make them breakfast, for which she'd likely lose her job.

Antoinette was well enough to go home now. As her mother led her away, I stood in the hospital's front doorway, watching them disappear once more into the rain.

6

Two days later, Nurse Emma appeared in the doorway to my office. The skin on her face, neck, and hands was dotted with fresh, angry red mosquito bites. I gestured for her to come in.

She took a seat and told me the story.

The mosquitoes had launched their attack the moment the medical team disembarked, terrorizing them in the tents outside Chalmette's one-room hospital, pursuing them into the cramped main building, and penetrating their bed nettings.

As she spoke, she scratched furiously at her arms, legs, and the tops of her feet.

"You need calamine," I said.

Despite her obvious suffering, she smiled mischievously. "Will you apply it, Doctor Whitaker?"

I hesitated, then nodded.

She fetched a bottle of pink calamine lotion, kicked off her shoes, peeled off her stockings, and hitched up her petticoats to reveal legs marred by welts. As I knelt beside her and applied the lotion with a cotton cloth, I felt the heat of her skin radiating through the fabric. I stopped where the petticoats gathered above the knee.

"How far up do they extend—the bites?" I asked.

"All the way, Doctor Whitaker."

I hesitated again.

"I can manage those parts myself, if you'd prefer," she said.

Nurse Emma was not only my colleague, but also, just then, my patient; professional decorum was called for more now than ever.

"That would probably be for the best," I said. "Stand up, and I'll attend to your neck and shoulders."

She slid off the table and turned her back to me. Her neck was even more ravaged than her legs, hot and mottled. After dabbing the cloth to her inflamed skin, I tried to lower her collar.

"Unbutton it," she said. "Or it won't go down."

I undid the buttons and slid the collar down several inches. The top of her back emerged—pale, freckled, and marred by red splotches that stood out starkly against her skin. I paused.

"It's bad," I said. "Calamine won't be enough. You'll need—"

"Let's start with that and see how it goes," she interrupted.

I felt a twinge of irritation at her attempt to override my professional recommendation. "Spirits of ammonia would be more effective," I said. "To reduce the swelling."

She glanced over her shoulder. "Will you apply the calamine to my back, Doctor Whitaker? Or shall I ask Doctor Broussard to do it?"

"I'll do it. But if your condition worsens by morning, please reconsider."

She nodded.

I applied the lotion, excused myself, and stepped out, irritated—at her for dismissing my advice and at myself for letting it bother me. I avoided her for the rest of the day, and by the time I decided to seek her out, she was already gone.

Before I left, I checked the tin in my coat pocket: only one pill remained. I'd need a dozen more to make it through to Thursday. I strolled to the medicine room at the end of the hall but stopped short when I saw Nurse Jean at her desk, eyes fixed on me like a cat's on a mouse.

"Yes?" she said.

"I—that is, I wanted to make sure Nurse Emma had returned the calamine lotion. For the mosquito bites."

She glanced at the bottle of pink liquid sitting conspicuously on the shelf.

"Right," I said. "Just wanted to be certain she'd remembered to put it back. There'll be others needing it soon."

Without waiting for her reply, I backed into the hallway. I clocked out for the day, stepped out into the rain, and made my way to the apothecary on Chartres Street.

7

The three-story Creole-American townhouse, with its cheery pink paint and white trim, had caught my eye more than once, though I'd never been inside.

When I stepped through the door, I was surprised to see a familiar face: Patience Dufilho, the woman I'd met in Jackson Square. She stood behind the counter, chatting with a young woman in a yellow dress and an orange tignon, the headwrap worn by many local black women since a law passed some years ago barred them from showing their hair in public.

Noticing me, Mrs. Dufilho smiled warmly and gave me a small wave. Her presence, along with the prospect of refilling my personal medicinal supplies, helped lift the pall that had hung over me since my argument with Nurse Emma.

The woman in yellow glanced at me, appeared to take me in, then returned to her conversation with Mrs. Dufilho.

While I waited, my gaze wandered over the staggering array of medicines and treatments on the shelves: ointments, tinctures, powders, pills, liniments, salves, balms—all neatly arranged and labeled.

As the woman in yellow departed, she paused in the doorway, turned to me, and smiled with honey-brown eyes and lips the color of pink rose petals.

"Evening, Sugar," she said. "How you doin'?"

I stood frozen, captivated, barely managing to mumble, "Good evening, Miss. Fine, thank you."

"That's real good," she said with a smile that melted my insides and made my scalp tingle. She stepped out, popped her umbrella, and receded into the rain-blurred distance.

I wasn't sure what it was about her that had struck me so acutely. After all, New Orleans was full of beautiful black women.

"That's Charlotte," Mrs. Dufilho said. "Quite the charmer, isn't she?"

"Indeed she is," I replied. "But what are you..."

"Doing here? My husband Louis hasn't been well. He's sleeping upstairs, so I've been manning the counter."

"Your husband?"

"Mr. Dufilho."

"Ah."

"This is his pharmacy. Dufilho's Pharmacy."

I glanced around and noticed the words *Dufilho's Pharmacy* in small gold-leaf lettering on the front window.

"Yes. Of course."

So that's where I knew the name from. I felt relieved to have solved that mystery.

Mrs. Dufilho and I chatted for a while as closing time approached, touching on the usual topics—the death and rot in the streets, the endless dreary rains, the difficulty of maintaining one's spirits during an epidemic.

Just before the apothecary's closing time, I selected a modest assortment of bottles, bundles, and tins—enough to suggest I hadn't come solely for the morphine pills—only to realize I was short on cash. Mrs. Dufilho graciously offered me a line of credit until the end of the month.

My day off was the first truly pleasant day I'd had in weeks. The ceiling refrained from leaking, allowing me a full night's sleep. I awoke to sunshine streaming through the window, descended cheerily to the cigar factory, where I savored my cigar and coffee in the front room, and found myself feeling more content than I had in some time.

Buoyed by this rare good mood, I decided it was time to move forward, as Mary Beth would have wanted me to. Nearly a year had passed since those terrible events in Wyoming, and I felt Nurse Emma might harbor at least some hint of affection for me, despite our differences. And so I resolved to ask her to join me for dinner and a show in the coming days.

The following morning, when I stepped through the hospital's front door, I was met not by the usual cacophony of nurses' chatter, patients' groans and echoing shrieks, but by a stark silence. The air was heavy, and a peculiar scent hung in it, ripe, like rotting fruit, with the faintest hint of wet metal.

I peered into the waiting room and found it eerily vacant. Dust motes pirouetted in the shafts of sunlight that fell across the legs of an upturned chair.

"Hello?" I called, my voice sounding oddly harsh in the hush.

There was no response.

I hurried down the corridor to Room 1, where I found an old woman with skin the color of parchment lying in her bed, eyes open but vacant. A fly crawled across her forehead.

"Ma'am?" I said.

I took her wrist to feel for a pulse, but the frigid skin beneath my fingertips told me everything. I pulled the sheet over her face.

A dull ache stirred in my chest. I moved on.

Another room, another lifeless patient: a teenage boy with the rough look of a dockworker, a crust of black vomit running from his lips, over his chin, and down his throat.

Panic shot through me.

"Emma?" I called out.

The only reply was the echo of my voice.

I hurried to Room 3. There, a young man lay rigid in the bed, his yellowed, bulging eyes staring blankly at the ceiling. Dried blood formed rust-red crusts at their corners.

Beside him, Nurse Jean sat slumped in a chair, her head tilted forward, her face veiled by long black hair that swayed gently in the air's eddies. Her white cap rested against her left shoe, where it had fallen.

"Nurse Jean?" I whispered. "Are you all right?"

I brushed aside her hair. Her face was marred by festering mosquito bites. I took her wrist to check for a pulse, but there was none.

I stood frozen, my mind grappling with what I'd seen—an eradication, a sweeping away of life.

This wasn't a hospital anymore. It was a morgue.

"Oh, my God," I whispered, backing away from Nurse Jean and the rigid man. "Emma!" I shouted, louder this time, the sound echoing through the empty halls.

I stumbled down the corridor and into the next room. There, Doctor Broussard lay sprawled across the bed. Plump, wriggling leeches clung to his arm, abdomen, and neck—he had tried to treat himself, but it was too late.

On the floor, a young boy in a long nightshirt lay splayed across the boards, one lifeless eye fixed on me, judging me for living. I tried to make sense of it: had Broussard dragged the boy from the bed to make room for himself?

Suddenly, I could barely breathe. I bent over, trying not to faint. When I'd regained myself, I sprinted down the hall to the staff room, desperate for any sign of life. It was deserted, except for a half-eaten sandwich on the table: a thin slice of pork between two slices of baguette. Emma's sandwich.

But where was she?

"Emmma!" I called out again.

The cold fear in my chest began to burn.

I dashed out of Saint Anne's, sunlight stabbing at my eyes as I stumbled into the street.

She was out there somewhere, alive. I had to believe it. I had to find her. A dreadful realization struck me: I had no idea where she lived. But her address would be in *there*, buried somewhere deep inside the hospital's files.

I returned to the entrance, froze, and stood trembling. Taking a deep breath, I stepped inside. Before entering the office, I went to the medicine room; the shelves were empty. Someone had already raided the supplies.

Ten hellish minutes later, armed with Emma's address, I reemerged and ran to her residence, a tenement building on Barracks Street. I raced up the stairs to the second floor and pounded on the door to room 21.

The manager, a stocky man in his forties with graying hair and a cigar clamped between his teeth, appeared on the landing. "Something I can help you with, mister?" he said.

"We have to check on Miss Smith," I blurted out. "Everyone at the hospital is dead. She might be inside, sick and in need of help."

He removed the cigar from his mouth with exasperating slowness. "And you are?"

"Hiram Whitaker. I'm a doctor at the hospital where she works."

"I'll check on her," he said. "You stay put."

I waited anxiously, heart pounding, as he disappeared into the apartment. A minute later, he reemerged.

"No sign of her," he said. "Bed's made. Room's empty, except for a bowl of fruit and a few garments. Looks like she packed up and left. Didn't even ask for her deposit."

"Could I take a look for myself? You might have missed something. It's—"

"No, you can't. You want to meddle in my tenants' affairs, then bring the police."

Frustration surged through me, but I kept my composure for Emma's sake.

"If you see her, please tell her to contact Doctor Whitaker, above the cigar factory on Levee Street."

"Sure."

I ran to the police station to report the deaths at Saint Anne's and file a missing person's report for Emma. The officer at the desk barely looked up from his paperwork as I recounted the horrors I'd seen and my fear that Nurse Emma was out there somewhere, sick or in danger. He scratched his nose and jotted a few notes.

"Yeah, we got a report about something down there," he said, stifling a yawn. "Look, Doc. We got six, seven hundred people dropping dead like flies around here every week. More than half the department's gone, either dead or skipped town. So, your little drama ain't the most interesting show in town right now."

The cold truth of it hit me: the police couldn't help.

I was on my own.

For a week, I visited every place Emma had ever mentioned —cafés, libraries, theaters—and found them all shuttered or abandoned. I wandered her favorite spots: parks, squares, the river's edge. I returned to her residence several times a day, but the manager always said the same thing: "No sign of her, Doc."

8

J.W. McFarland's residence in the American Quarter was a white two-story mansion surrounded by lush gardens and an ornate cast-iron fence in the elaborate style currently all the rage—and no doubt wildly expensive. I had little hope of finding him at home, as most of the city's elite had fled the epidemic. Still, it was worth a try. I knocked.

After a brief wait, the door opened, and a petite black woman in a crisp blue dress appeared. I introduced myself as an associate of Dr. McFarland's and said that I wished to speak with him on a matter of grave importance. She nodded and led me into the front parlor, where she left me to wait.

As I sank into the plump floral-upholstered chair, my eyes were drawn to a black casket resting on a stand before the fireplace, and I wondered whether it was already occupied, or still awaiting its eternal tenant.

After some time, I stood and paced the room, taking in its opulence: imported furniture, porcelain miniatures, a velvet settee. I paused before a gilt-framed mirror to study the gaunt figure staring back at me. Drawn features, weary eyes, clothes hanging loosely on an angular frame: was this what the past several months had done to me?

An hour passed before the servant returned with a tray of tea and toast. "Please follow me, Mr. Whitaker," she said. "Doctor McFarland will be down shortly."

I followed her into the back parlor and sank into an even plusher chair. Parched by then, I sipped the peppermint tea gratefully.

Twenty minutes later, heavy footsteps sounded on the stairs. My heart quickened—I thought it must be McFarland. But instead, a large black woman in a cream-colored muslin gown passed the parlor entrance, heading toward the front door.

Another ten minutes passed before McFarland himself strolled in and dropped into a chair across from me, propping an ankle on one knee.

"Come to apologize, Whicket?"

"Apologize, sir?"

"For that childish outburst the other day, down in the square."

He shook his head in evident disgust.

I clenched my fists.

"No. I... you've no doubt heard about what happened at Saint Anne's?"

"That boy on the whipping post was one of mine. Caught red-handed, plotting a revolt with some others down from LaPlace. They'd have slit our throats and disemboweled the lot of us, women and children first. You backed the wrong team, Whicket."

I held back my retort—that in a civilized society, we try a man in a court of law and jail him if he's found guilty, not debase ourselves with barbarism.

"So you haven't heard about—" I began.

"Of course I've heard about it. But let's get back to my point. Our profession relies on respect. You can't expect people to respect you if you make a fool of yourself in the public square. When you dishonor yourself, you dishonor the whole profession. That's why I assumed you came to apologize. To me, and to the entire medical institution."

I opened my mouth to protest, then closed it again. Fighting a surge of rage, I felt short of breath.

"You know, then," I said, "that Nurse Jean and Doctor Broussard died of the fever. That everyone at the hospital has either died or fled."

He nodded, then raised his eyebrows, as if to say, And what of it?

"Yet here I am," I continued, "ready—eager, even—to continue my work, no matter the risk. Shouldn't that count for something?"

He shook his head. "You and I are men of science, Whicket. As such, we understand the necessity—the moral imperative—of slavery."

My throat tightened. Was I choking on something?

"You'll have noticed," he continued, "that certain classes of men don't fall victim to yellow fever. The wealthy Creole. The American. The negro. It strikes down only those weakened by moral or financial impoverishment. And yet, despite suffering from both, the negro never gets yellow fever. Do you know why that is, Whicket?"

I swallowed hard and found my breath. "It's Whitaker."

"I'll tell you why. Because slavery makes them strong. The strong survive, the weak die. It's natural law. Through slavery, we've bred the strongest race on Earth—the American negro. And for that, they'll owe us their eternal gratitude and an eternal debt."

My grip tightened on the armrest.

"And how will they repay us that debt?" McFarland asked.

"I don't know," I lied.

"Of course you do. They shall repay it through slavery."

The servant entered with fresh tea. McFarland uncapped a silver flask and poured a splash into his teacup.

"Thank you, Muriel," he said. Then, turning to me, "Whiskey?"

I shook my head.

"A man of tender constitution," he said. "Why am I not surprised?" He slapped Muriel's backside as she turned to leave. "Now, where were we?"

"You were saying moral and financial impoverishment lead to yellow fever."

"Yes, exactly that."

"Then what moral impoverishment killed Doctor Broussard or Nurse Jean? Or children?"

"You're being a jackass, Whicket. I'm trying to knock some sense into that alleged brain of yours, but you're making it damn difficult."

"I'm just—"

"You're here," he snapped, "because you don't want to fail your residency, and you need my help. And I'm trying to help you, God knows why. But you're pigheaded. You're a Northerner who doesn't understand our peculiar institution. Yet for some reason you want to practice medicine here. But our medicine isn't the same as yours. Our diseases aren't the same, our people aren't. That's why your degree from the University of New York is as worthless as a nun's tit here, and why you must complete your residency in New Orleans if you wish to be licensed and practice here. And now the hospital where you worked is shuttered, because everyone there has either dropped dead or run away, in a most cowardly and despicable fashion. Do I have my facts straight?"

I nodded, though I was fairly certain Emma was neither cowardly nor despicable.

"Then you're in a pickle, Whicket."

"I thought I might reopen Saint Anne's as resident doctor, finish my residency, and then—"

McFarland shook his head. "That's not how it works, you dunderhead. You can't supervise your own residency. You need a licensed physician to sign off on your work."

"Then post me at Charity."

"If it were possible, it'd have to be unpaid."

"Unpaid? But why?"

"The Board of Health won't release the funds for any new posts. Maybe next legislative session. But there's no telling when that'll be."

"But you're the Director of the Board—"

"I work for the city, Whicket. The mayor and council call the shots, and they're all Whigs who'd sooner see the poor and the immigrants die than let them live to vote Democrat."

"What about Saint Anne's? Won't they want to reopen it as soon as possible?"

"Haven't the faintest clue. The church runs it. It's not my business. I doubt they're in a rush to reopen, after what happened."

"But if they did—"

"They wouldn't rehire you."

"But why?"

"Because your anti-Catholic views are no secret in this town. All your whining and whimpering about prayer and crucifixes doesn't set well with that crowd. And why should it? Charity's a Catholic-run hospital, too. I doubt they'd hire you even for no pay."

"Then what am I supposed to do? There must be something."

He poured another splash of whiskey into his tea, sipped it, and regarded me over the cup's rim.

"Go back to Philadelphia or New York, or wherever it is you came from."

The two places I could never return to.

"What about General Hospital?" I asked.

"Same as Charity. There aren't any funds. They might give you a chance, despite your reputation as a radical. But they can't pay you."

"Radical?"

"Atheist. Northerner."

Exasperated, I rose from my chair. McFarland stood as well.

"Thank you for your time," I said.

"I've enjoyed our little chat, Whicket. Muriel!"

9

Walking home from McFarland's house in the early evening, I came to Canal Street. It was desolate, save for a few prowling wild dogs. I kept my distance and turned toward the river, where I encountered a small caravan of drays piled high with human bodies.

I stopped beneath a cottonwood and watched as two black men lifted the body of a white woman from one of the drays, laid her on a wheelbarrow and pushed it to the end of a narrow wharf, where they dumped her into the river. She disappeared beneath the surface, then popped up. As her head bobbed in the filthy water, her dead, yellow eyes settled on me—just as those of the man on the whipping post had, just as the dead boy's in Saint Anne's had.

I closed my eyes and pressed my hands to my face, trying to erase the image this scene stirred in my memory: that of my infant sister's baptism, which I'd attended along the icy shore of the East River. But I still saw the startled, wide-eyed look she'd given me when the priest lifted her head from the freezing water. So I pressed harder, until her face dissolved into a white flash behind my eyelids.

As I trudged homeward, the distant boom of cannons, the steady clop-clop of passing funeral wagons, and the mournful wailing of the bereaved assaulted my senses.

Uncertain what to do next, I considered writing home for funds. My father didn't have much, but more than I did. I could offer to repay him, with interest. But as I paused before the window of an abandoned shop and caught my reflection in the dirty glass, I thought, *You must never put yourself in that murderer's debt.*

I wandered on until I realized I'd passed my apartment and drifted down to the brothels across from the French Market. Standing on the sticky sidewalk before a row of shuttered butcher stalls, I took in the vast expanse of whoredom arrayed before me, stretching from one end of the block to the other. There were women black as coal, white as snow, and every shade in between. Some were fat as pumpkins, others skinny as brooms. A few looked older than my mother might've been, had she lived; others, younger than my sister was the day she died. Most looked healthy, vibrant even. If moral failing led to sickness, you wouldn't know it here.

My eyes settled on a girl no older than ten, provocatively dressed and leaning against the frame of an open doorway. Behind her, in the shadows of a staircase, stood a woman whose face was garishly caked in makeup and whose left breast was completely exposed. The little girl raised her hand to beckon me.

Horrified she'd think me capable of such a thing, I turned to leave. But before I could take a single step, something struck me in the back of my head, and the last thing I saw through a flash of white light was that little girl's wicked grin.

Night had fallen by the time I awoke to find myself lying on the sidewalk, my head half-submerged in the gutter's muck. Groaning in pain, I forced myself upright and gripped a lamppost for support.

I checked my belongings—they were gone. My hat, my watch, my wallet. My gold wedding band—the last vestige of Mary Beth.

I reached back to find my hair matted with blood. Whoever struck me had landed the blow in the exact spot I'd hit on the cobblestones in the square.

Across the road, shadows shifted. They were watching me.

Despite taking double my usual dose of morphine the night before—it was all I had left, and I meant to make the most of it—I awoke with a pounding headache, as if a railroad spike had been driven through my skull. My body ached all over; every joint felt stiff and brittle. Even the slightest movement brought sharp waves of nausea.

Still, I forced myself out of bed.

My only plan beyond wandering the streets in search of Emma was to visit the apothecary and procure more morphine. I hadn't paid my bill, but I'd plead with Mrs. Dufilho for an extension.

During my breakfast of cigar and coffee, Javier, a Haitian roller, glanced up from his work.

"You look bad this morning, Monsieur Whitaker," he said, his voice carrying that comforting Creole lilt. "White as a dead man, dead as a white man," he added with a wink. "Let me get you another coffee, nice and black. Make you feel better."

I rose stiffly and steadied myself against the chair.

"*Merci,* Javier. But I've got business to attend to."

"You found another job?"

"Something like that."

I emerged onto the banquette and opened my new umbrella against the downpour—which had returned with a vengeance after a brief, teasing lull—and made my way toward the apothecary.

Rounding the corner onto Chartres Street, I stopped in my tracks. A covered freight wagon stood out front. Workers passed in and out of the building, carrying wooden crates and shipping trunks, loading them onto the wagon. I crossed to the other side of the street and watched from the shelter of the Slave Exchange arcade. A sign on the apothecary window read Closed for Business.

My heart sank. Had the Dufilhos already left? If so, what had become of their medicinal supplies?

Then, through the rain-fogged glass, I spotted Mrs. Dufilho inside, directing the workers. I dashed across the street and into the apothecary. She noticed me and offered a rueful smile.

"Mrs. Dufilho, what's happening here?"

"Mr. Whitaker, what a pleasant surprise," she said, stepping from behind the counter and pulling me into a brief embrace. "My dear Louis has departed."

"Departed?"

"It happened a few days ago. One moment he was recovering, the next... his heart simply ceased to beat."

"I'm very sorry for your loss, Mrs. Dufilho."

"I knew this day would come, but the pain is truly unbearable."

As she spoke, I became aware of a tall, well-dressed black man standing near the door to the courtyard behind the apothecary, watching me with what appeared to be intense interest.

I cleared my throat. "Those crates, then...?"

"I'm returning to New York. They contain only what I can't bear to leave behind."

The man's scrutiny was unwavering. It seemed as if he knew me, or thought he did.

"And the apothecary stock?" I asked.

"I've arranged for Charity Hospital to take possession of it. You know how stretched they are these days."

"Of course. But, I wonder, have they already inventoried the stronger medicines—the narcotics and such?"

The man by the rear doorway finally turned away, apparently satisfied he didn't know me after all. He walked further into the courtyard, retrieved a key from his vest pocket, unlocked a door, and disappeared inside.

"No, Doctor Whitaker," Mrs. Dufilho said. "They don't intend to inventory anything. Charity is sending someone tomorrow to collect it all."

"Ah. Then..."

She gently grasped my hand. "I heard what happened at the hospital. I also heard someone made off with all the supplies. You must have patients under your care who are in desperate need, with no way to treat them. Is that right?"

"Yes," I said. "That is... no."

"No? Then what is it you..."

"I don't have any patients. They've all died. It's I who am in desperate need."

"I see," she said, nodding. "Then, come with me."

She led me into the courtyard and knocked on the door. After a moment, the man reappeared.

"Yes, ma'am?"

"Jerome, this is Doctor Whitaker, a dear friend of mine. Doctor Whitaker, this is Jerome de La Chance, my slave."

"Pleasure to meet you, Doctor," he said.

"Your slave?" I asked.

"Yes," she replied. "My slave."

"But I assumed..."

"Jerome, Doctor Whitaker is in immediate need of medicine. Please escort him upstairs and locate the box marked *Opiates*. It contains the morphine. Give him as much as he requires."

The mere mention of the word opiates revived my spirits.

"Yes, ma'am," he said with a slight bow. "Doctor Whitaker, if you'll follow me."

I followed him into the building and up the staircase to the second floor, where crates of various sizes were stacked, some open, others sealed.

"Here we are," he said, kneeling in front of one of them. "Opiates. Are you taking these for your practice, Doctor?"

We held each other's gaze for a moment.

"Or for yourself?"

"I..."

"Do you need something now, to tide you over?"

"Yes. I'm afraid I do."

"Very well. Do you prefer pills or the syringe?"

"You have syringes? That is—I don't wish to be a bother."

The syringe was a new European contrivance; I was surprised the Dufilhos should already have some.

"No bother at all, Doctor. I believe we have a few around here somewhere, still in the box." He scanned the labels on various crates. "Here we are. We'll have you feeling better in no time. Why don't you take a seat? Make yourself comfortable."

I eased into the chair and tilted my head back. A solitary fly perched on the ceiling. I watched it for a moment, envying its simple life.

Jerome prepared the morphine in a small dish.

"I believe the usual dose is five milligrams," he said. "We'll fix you up with ten, just to make sure you're well taken care of."

He drew the liquid into the syringe and laid it on the table.

"Make a fist, Doctor."

I complied. He tapped my arm, searching for the vein. "Low on blood," he said. "I'd recommend garlic, onions, and peppers." He pulled a handkerchief from his vest and tied it around my arm, then tapped again. "There we go."

He took the syringe, gave it a final flick, slid the needle in, and pressed down on the plunger. The effect was immediate. The pain—of both body and mind—softened, liquefied, and drained away. I don't know how long I drifted, cradled by warmth and relief, before I opened my eyes to see Jerome seated beside me, watching quietly.

"Better now?" he said.

"Indeed, yes. Thank you."

"Good."

"You know," I said, "I'm surprised the Dufilhos have a slave. I first met Mrs. Dufilho at a whipping, over in the square. From our conversation, I took it she disapproved of it."

"Oh, she does. And you, Doctor?"

"Disapprove of it? Of course I do. It's an abomination. But it won't last long, believe me."

"It's in the Bible," he said, as if that settled the matter.

"All the more abominable."

"I've been the Dufilhos' slave for years. I belonged to the previous owners, too."

"No man can own another."

"They do here. But the Dufilhos have always let me do as I please. Mostly I just work. They tried to free me a few years ago, but the law of '52 put an end to that."

"Will you travel to New York with Madam Dufilho?"

He shook his head. "Slaves can't leave Louisiana. Wouldn't want to, anyway."

"But why could you possibly want to stay?"

"My sister, Arabella. She's a slave too. But it's not like it is here with the Dufilhos. I have to stay here to protect her. From her master."

"I understand you doing everything you can..." My voice hitched, and I paused to collect myself. "For your sister."

"Thank you."

"If I might ask, what sort of treatment does he subject her to?"

"You know. The usual things the Devil does. Punches her in the face, kicks her in the ribs when she's down.

Whips her when he's in the mood for blood. Never touches her belly, though."

"Is that because…"

He nodded.

"I'm sorry," I said. "I truly am."

"She says she'd rather be dead sometimes, than live that life any longer."

"Her master sounds like a monster. I understand why you could never leave her behind."

"You're right about that, Doctor Whitaker. If there's one thing true about J.W. McFarland, it's that he's a monster."

10

Mrs. Dufilho and I sat in her private parlor on the third floor, just off the master bedroom. She had left Jerome downstairs to oversee the movers.

"Sell Jerome to me," I said. "You'll have to sell him to someone when you leave. So why not me? He can remain here if he wants. And rent me this building. It will have to be on credit, but once I'm turning a profit, I'll pay you the back rent—with generous interest." The words spilled out of me in such a torrent that I briefly wondered whether Jerome had spiked the morphine with cocaine.

When I finished my pitch, Mrs. Dufilho regarded me with a calm smile, and I dared hope it meant she was amenable to my proposition.

"I'm afraid that's impossible," she said, her smile fading.

"But why?"

"Do you possess the proper licenses? To practice medicine? To operate a pharmacy?"

"Not yet," I confessed. "But soon."

"And how soon is 'soon'?"

"I don't know. But I'll find a way. I promise."

"And if you do find a way, do you have the necessary funds? To pay rent, to purchase equipment, to restock the medicines?"

I shut my eyes briefly, frustrated by her skepticism. Opening them, I said, "I do not."

"Then—"

"I swear to you, Mrs. Dufilho, on my honor—once I've established my practice, I'll pay you."

She gazed out the window for some time.

Fearful she was searching for a way to let me down gently, I said, "What about Jerome? What are your plans for him? He told me he had no idea what would become of him once you leave. Since you can't legally free him, who better to sell him to than someone who despises slavery as much as you do?"

Her continued silence told me the truth: she hadn't made any real plans for his future.

"You can't just leave him here," I said. "The authorities will seize him as abandoned property and auction him off to the highest bidder. Who knows what might become of him then?"

She looked out through the rain-streaked window to the Slave Exchange across the street. "I'd hoped my lawyer, Mr. Bradford, might find a satisfactory solution. I must give him time."

I leaned forward. "But I'm offering you a satisfactory solution right now."

"How do you intend to acquire the necessary supplies—the medicines, the equipment? Most suppliers won't extend credit to someone in your particular... straits."

"If you could leave me only the most essential medicines."

"Rather than donate them to Charity Hospital, which is in such dire need?"

"Not all of it. Just enough to help me get started. After all, had your husband not..."

"Had he not passed away? Then the medicines would have remained here anyway and not gone to Charity? Is that what you mean to say?"

"Yes, Mrs. Dufilho."

She laid a hand on my knee, and for a moment, I thought she might agree to my requests. But she withdrew it abruptly and returned her gaze to the window.

"Regrettably, dear Hiram, there remains a far more insurmountable hurdle to your well-meaning aspirations."

"Hurdle, Mrs. Dufilho?"

"I wasn't Louis Dufilho's first wife, you see. He was married before, to a rather unpleasant woman named Sarah. They had three children—Clarence, Peter, and Bethany—each as dreadful as their mother."

I considered her meaning. The full implication soon struck me: "Sarah owns half the building," I said. "And she'll want to put it up for sale."

"Exactly so. And ever since my dear Louis first showed signs of frailty a year ago, Sarah has maintained a lawyer here in New Orleans to keep an eye on us and safeguard her interests."

"Perhaps she'd agree to my rental proposal. I'd gladly pay above the going rate."

She shook her head. "Sarah will demand a lump sum from an immediate sale. And if I object, she'll sue and attempt to take everything."

Before I could respond, a knock came at the door, two triplets followed by an eighth note.

"Come in, Jerome," Mrs. Dufilho called.

He entered and cast a glance between us. "Movers are done for the day, ma'am. Everything's locked up downstairs."

"Thank you, Jerome."

"How are you feeling, Doctor Whitaker? You look... pale. Did I get the dose wrong?"

I shook my head. "I feel fine, thank you."

"Have a seat," Mrs. Dufilho said. "What we've been discussing concerns you as much as it does us."

Jerome sat. "Is it about what's going to happen to this place after you leave?"

"That, and your future," she replied. "Doctor Whitaker wishes to rent the building for his own use, but I've explained the situation with Sarah and the children."

He crossed his arms and nodded. "Mm-hmm."

"Sarah's lawyer, Mr. Duchamp, will no doubt have heard of my husband's passing, if not yet, then soon. And he'll demand—"

"Excuse me," Jerome said. "Mr. Duchamp? You mean Alex Duchamp?"

"Yes. Do you know him?"

Jerome nodded. "He's one of Marie's regulars. Comes in for a haircut and a shave."

"How interesting," Mrs. Dufilho said. "How long has he been going to Marie?"

"About ten years now."

"Then she must know rather much about Mr. Duchamp."

"Oh, she knows everything there is to know about him."

Some days later, I learned Alex Duchamp had fallen ill and left the city. In his letter to Mrs. Dufilho, he made it clear he'd be forced to remain away until the miasma cleared: several months, most likely.

Curious about this providential turn of events, I asked Mrs. Dufilho about it.

"Jerome works part-time at Marie Laveau's salon," she said. "As a hairdresser."

"Marie Laveau? The voodoo priestess?"

"Yes, that's right."

"She's the hairdresser Jerome works for?"

"She's most fond of Jerome, and I believe she'd do anything for him."

I had more questions, but decided, for now, to leave them unasked.

Mrs. Dufilho and I struck an agreement on a six-month lease. After that, we'd have to devise new arrangements. Sarah couldn't be kept in the dark forever.

Now, the challenge before me was to find a way to practice medicine and operate an apothecary without the proper licenses.

* * *

The following week, after Mrs. Dufilho had departed for New York, Jerome and I sat on a bench on the wharf, watching quarantine officers board a cargo ship moored in the river. The late August evening air was stifling and stank of death and burning pitch.

"I guess you don't favor the idea," Jerome said.

We'd been discussing our respective burdens: the mistreatment of his sister Arabella, and my need to secure a medical license from the Board, the obvious nexus being J.W. McFarland. Jerome had suggested—jokingly, I assumed, though I wasn't quite sure—that killing the man would be the simplest solution to our troubles.

"Murder's not really my cup of tea," I said, after giving the notion some thought. "And even if McFarland were gone, there would be someone else to take his place. The Board wouldn't change. The rules wouldn't change. And someone else would own Arabella. Possibly someone just as cruel."

"If we don't do something, he's going to kill her," Jerome said. "I can't accept that."

"You don't suppose your friend Marie Laveau could intervene? The way she did with Sarah's lawyer?"

"She won't meddle with McFarland. He's too dangerous. He's like an octopus—arms everywhere, hands in everything. She could cut off seven of 'em, he'd still strangle her with the eighth."

"I see."

Somehow, I found it easy to picture McFarland as a wicked, mustachioed mollusk.

"What if we just opened up shop?" Jerome said. "Treat people and sell medicine. No license, no framed paper on the wall. Most of the other doctors are dead or gone. I bet people would still come in."

The idea had a certain charm, even if it was unreasonable.

"Breaking the regulations would only ruin my record," I said. "Once things get back to normal, the Board might deny me the licenses. Even if I completed my residency."

"Suppose you brought in a licensed doctor to work at your practice and supervise you for the rest of your residency? Have him sign off on your work."

"I'd still have to pay him," I said. "And I still need to earn a living."

"Or," he said, "you could pay McFarland to turn a blind eye. After three months, he signs your papers, saying he supervised you."

As the setting sun cast a fiery glow over the river, shouts erupted on the deck of the cargo ship, something about the filth and degradation of the Americans.

"First you said we should kill him. Now you suggest we pay him?"

"Yes, exactly."

"At least your ideas are becoming less criminal and less violent, if only slightly."

"I want him dead. As violently as possible."

"Even if he could be bribed, I don't have the money."

A brawl broke out on the ship's deck. The crack of a fist meeting flesh echoed across the water, followed by the splash of a man plunging into it.

"I do," Jerome said.

"You have money?"

"You think I've been working for nothing all these years?"

"But you're a slave."

"Marie Laveau pays me. The Dufilhos paid me. My expenses have been minimal. No rent, no grocery bill. I don't drink, don't smoke, don't chase women. Lived at the Dufilho place for twenty years. I like my little room in the back, the sound of crickets and the fountain at night. If you let me stay there and help with the doctoring, I'll give you enough to pay off McFarland. You won't owe it back. We'll call it rent payment."

As the last sliver of sun dipped below the horizon, the men on the quarantine boat struggled to haul their crewmate from the water. The smoke covering the surface, only moments ago glowing a deep burnt orange, turned purple, then black.

"What do you mean, 'help with the doctoring'?"

"It's not easy to pull a tooth or amputate a leg by yourself."

"You helped Doctor Dufilho with those things?"

"I did. And I'll help you too, if the pay's right," he said, patting me on the knee. "I figure McFarland'll take five hundred dollars. Start with two, then let him haggle you up to five."

"You really have that much?"

"Yes, sir."

11

McFarland's drawing room felt different this time. My new-found knowledge of the depth of his cruelty filled the space with disquiet despite the soft glow of evening light filtering through the windows—and the absence of the casket. After nearly an hour of waiting, McFarland entered, his face flushed, shirt rumpled. The smell of sex wafted from him, nearly overpowering the pungent aromas of cigar smoke and fatty beef lingering in the air. He settled into a chair across from me.

"To what do I owe this new displeasure, Whicket? I thought you'd have scurried back to Massachusetts by now."

Jerome and I had rehearsed this moment, and I was de-termined to play my role effectively, despite my grave doubts about my acting abilities. I straightened in my seat and smoothed my trousers.

"I've secured a six-month lease on the Dufilho property. I intend to continue operating the apothecary and practic-ing medicine."

He raised an eyebrow. "Neither of which you're licensed to do. Nor likely to become so. What's your purpose here?"

"To offer a proposition. A financial one."

He leaned back, lacing his fingers behind his head. "Proceed, Whicket."

"Two hundred dollars to supervise the final three months of my residency. You'll check in as you see fit—to review the records, treatments, prescriptions, whatever you like. At the end, you'll sign off as my supervising physician."

"You're offering me a bribe."

I shook my head.

"No surprise, coming from you," he said. "A desperate ploy by a desperate man."

"I'm offering you a fee for your time, expertise, and authority. That is all."

"Bribes are illegal, Whicket. What you're proposing is a crime."

"No one here is offering anyone a bribe, Doctor McFarland."

"That's rich."

"I can offer you three hundred dollars. Not a penny more."

He lit a pipe and expelled a cloud of rum-scented smoke. "Suppose I accept this fee, and enter it into your record as the attempted bribe that it is. How would you like that?"

I nodded. "Four hundred, then. To ensure our mutual discretion and satisfaction."

Jerome had instructed me to use those exact words.

McFarland blew another cloud of smoke in my direction, as if to obscure my existence from his view.

"And if I report this four hundred dollars to the Medical Board, the Board of Health, the City Council, the Police

Department? Would that too lead to our mutual discretion and satisfaction?"

I stood. "Five hundred dollars. Take it or leave it. I don't care. Report this alleged *bribe* to whomever you wish."

His eyes flashed. "For the love of Christ, Whicket, sit down."

I hesitated long enough to suggest careful consideration, then lowered myself back into the chair.

He leaned forward. "Prove you've got the cash, and I'm sure we can make a satisfactory arrangement."

I tossed my stuffed billfold onto the table.

He swiveled toward the doorway. "Muriel!" he called out. "Bring the good whiskey!"

12

I stood in the master suite and turned slowly in place, feeling small in the vastness of the room. Smoky rays of evening light slanted through the balcony windows, casting a warm golden-orange hue over the few belongings Mrs. Dufilho had left behind: a chair, a desk, a chamber pot, and the bed, an immense four-poster that dwarfed the dimensions of my cramped little room on Levee Street.

I opened the French doors and stepped out onto the balcony to take in the street below. It was mostly deserted, but for the occasional figure staggering along the banquette, sidestepping the filth. The stench of feces and rotting garbage wafted up—the municipal garbage service having ceased months ago, and the hotels, taverns, and boarding houses now dumping their refuse and sewage directly into the alleys from where it spilled into the streets.

I retreated inside.

A moment later, Jerome appeared in the doorway.

"Come in," I said.

"Big bed. For just one person."

"I've been thinking, Jerome. It seems a shame for you to stay out back. We'll only need half the second floor. If you'd like, you can take the other half…"

He shook his head. "I like it fine out there. Lived in that shack since I was twelve years old. I like my privacy."

"Since you were twelve? By yourself?"

"Yes, sir."

"What about your parents?"

"They were slaves. I'm a slave. I lost track of them when I was five and Arabella was two. Took care of her until they sent us apart."

"You're not a slave anymore, Jerome."

"I am. I'm your slave."

"Please don't say that."

"But it's true."

"I won't have any slaves living on my property."

"This isn't your property, Doctor Whitaker. It's Patience Dufilho's."

"As far as I'm concerned, you're an associate. If you intend to work here."

He nodded. "Like I said, it's hard for a man to cut off a leg without someone holding down the man it's attached to."

"Good. Incidentally, how much did the Dufilhos pay you?"

"Dollar a day for twelve hours' work."

"Then I'll pay you two dollars, once we've got some cash coming in. Until then, keep a record of what I owe you."

He nodded but lingered in the doorway, brow furrowed as he scratched his chin.

"What is it?" I asked.

"You're going to need someone else, too. Front desk, pharmacy sales, appointments. Someone to hold down the fort while you and I are upstairs treating patients. I have customers at Marie's, so I can't always be here. Mrs. Dufilho took care of those things before. You'll need someone."

"Do you have anyone in mind?"

He hesitated. "No. You'll have to run a notice in the paper."

I nodded.

"There are other things I did for the Dufilhos," he said. "I could do them for you, too, if you like."

"What sort of things?"

"Housework. Cooking. Cleaning. You know—slave work."

"You won't do any of those things if you'll call it that."

"Someone has to," he said, glancing around the room. "Seeing as how you don't have a wife. Or even a girlfriend, far as I can tell. Do you?"

I shook my head.

"You like women, though, right?"

"Of course I do. Don't be ridiculous."

"You never know."

"I had a wife."

His expression softened, and he wisely let it go.

Jerome and I knelt on the floor, digging through boxes. I opened one and found three burlap bags. Inside each were paper packets with labels on them.

"Balsam of Peru, Orris root, Calamus root, Patchouli leaves, Clary sage, Tonka beans, Khus-khus," I read aloud. "Jerome?"

He looked up from the box he was rummaging through. "Yes?"

"What is this?" I held up a packet.

"What's what?"

"Khus-khus."

"Haitian name for vetiver root."

"It's not some sort of voodoo root, is it?"

"Up to you what you do with it, Doc."

"That's not an answer to my question."

"Anyone could use any kind of root in voodoo, if they wanted to."

"Could they use a sarsaparilla root?"

He shrugged. "I'm no root expert, Doctor Whitaker."

"And what about these other things? Balsam of Peru? Tonka beans? What are they?"

"Botanicals. Plants."

"But what are they doing in an apothecary's stock? That's what I'm struggling to comprehend."

"I believe those are used in sachet powders, mostly."

"Sachet? Do you mean gris-gris bags?"

"Not the same thing. But like I said—"

"Are any of these botanicals used medicinally?"

"Some are."

I dug further into the bag and found a folded piece of paper listing recipes using the bag's contents.

"Adam and Eve Powder. Fast Luck Powder. Git-You-a-Man Powder," I read aloud.

I glanced at Jerome, but he had nothing to add; he merely continued rummaging through the box in front of him.

I opened another bag and found more labeled packets: *Sandalwood, Gum Benzoin, Tobacco, Chili, Master Root.* The recipe sheet listed *Confusion Powder, Basic Love Powder,* and *Jinx Removing Powder.*

"Jerome," I said, holding up the paper. "These are voodoo recipes. There isn't any doubt about it."

"Is that right?"

"You know perfectly well they are. Tell me what they're doing here."

"Mr. Dufilho sold them downstairs in the pharmacy. That's all I know."

"These are not legitimate medicines. Why would he sell such things?"

"People buy them, so Mr. Dufilho sold them. It's a business. Supply and demand. There's plenty demand, so he supplied."

"I bet he used these quack powders to treat himself. And look where it got him."

Jerome sat upright. "Mr. Dufilho treated himself with mercury, arsenic, and leeches. And look where *that* got him."

"This is nonsense. I won't have any voodoo powders in my apothecary, business or not. Do what you want with them. Give them to Marie Laveau, for all I care. But remove them from these premises."

"I'll see they're taken care of."

* * *

The next morning, a Saturday, Jerome caught me regarding myself in the mirror above the soda dispenser.

"You're not bad-looking, Doctor Whitaker. But you could use some work."

I turned toward him, feeling a flicker of embarrassment at being called "not bad-looking" by another man. Yet Jerome had an undeniable air of style, and I couldn't help but be curious as to his meaning.

"Work?" I said.

"That hair of yours. That beard. *Sincèrement?* This isn't 1843. And those clothes, those shoes? No one's going to let you lay a hand on their body if you're wearing those old things. Come by Marie's and we'll fix you up and bring you right into the 1850s."

Later that day, after we'd made some progress setting up the apothecary display cases, Jerome ushered me into Marie Laveau's salon on Saint Ann Street. He led me past tables cluttered with dolls fashioned from straw and human hair, jars of roots and bones, gris-gris bags, and vials of shimmering liquid. In the back, people chattered in French and various African dialects, punctuated by bursts of laughter and the rhythmic snip of scissors. Women in vibrant headwraps bustled between barber chairs, tending to clients. The whole place struck me as profoundly exotic, more than a little overwhelming, yet undeniably stimulating.

A mulatto woman caught my eye. She wore a long indigo dress, and a red-and-yellow tignon framed her strikingly beautiful face. Thick strands of amber, green, and blue beads hung around her neck, draping over her bosom.

Noticing a cane topped with a silver snake's head leaning against the wall, I knew this must be Marie Laveau.

Jerome approached her and whispered something in her ear. She turned to me with a warm smile.

"Monsieur Whitaker," she said, "what a profound delight! We have been expecting you for a very long time."

Surprised by her enthusiastic friendliness, I could only manage a nod and a tip of my hat.

"Over here," Jerome said, gesturing toward a row of chairs. "It's time we made you look like a proper doctor."

I went over and took a seat. Jerome set a tin basin on the counter.

"What did she mean by that—'expecting me a long time'?"

Jerome shrugged. "Just being friendly, I guess."

He took my hat, draped a towel over my shoulders, and began snipping away at my beard.

Unsatisfied with his answer, I asked, "Did you tell her we were coming?"

"Can't remember. Must have, if she was expecting you."

Something about the whole thing unsettled me, but I decided to let it go.

Jerome worked quickly, and I was startled when he began shaving away what remained of my beard.

"I'd imagined something more like a trim," I said. "To tidy things up."

"We won't know what to do with that hair of yours until we see your bone structure," he replied. "Assuming you've got any."

"Bone structure?"

"The shape of your face."

"You sound more like a surgeon than a barber."

"Bit of both, I reckon."

"I assume you have a barber's license, if not one for surgery."

"A man's got gangrene in his leg, I chop it off to save him. What's the law going to do, make me sew it back on? Same for beards. Ah, here we go. There's some structure here, after all."

His fingertips traced the contours of my jaw, then ascended to my earlobes, one of which he gently tugged. The gesture felt surprisingly intimate, yet not entirely unpleasant. He placed two fingers beneath my chin and tilted my head back.

"Hiding that cleft chin of yours from the ladies all this time," he said. "You ought to be ashamed of yourself."

He wrapped my face in a hot towel, and I must have drifted off. When I awoke, the towel was gone, and Marie Laveau stood before me.

"*Très beau,*" she said. She ran her fingers along my mustache, tip to tip. "Apply the wax *comme ça,* Jerome. Then curl." She demonstrated the motion with a delicate twist. "Soon, monsieur, you will be the most handsome man in New Orleans, and I shall insist you belong to me, and only to me."

I felt my face flush.

She gave my arm a playful tap, winked, and glided away to another client.

Jerome took a straight razor and began scraping away the remaining stubble. When he was done, he rinsed my face and wrapped it in an ice-cold towel. The shock of it jolted my senses, sharpening the sounds and smells of the bustling shop. He removed the towel and slapped my cheeks with a spicy astringent. It burned, and for a moment, I felt more alive than I had in a long time.

He turned me toward the mirror and rested his fingertips on my cheeks. "We'll get some food in you and fill out these shadows. Soon enough, the ladies and gentlemen will flock to Whitaker's Pharmacy just to catch a glimpse of you."

"They'll flock to us when we provide superior medical care," I said, eyeing my reflection.

The transformation truly was remarkable.

"One thing I learned from the Dufilhos, and from Marie, too," Jerome said, "doctoring's a sales job. Prettier the salesman, prettier the sales."

"Marie Laveau's not a doctor."

He shrugged, picked up a copper spray bottle, misted my hair, and combed it into sections, securing each with a spring-loaded contraption.

"What are those things for?" I asked.

"Fixing you up."

He began trimming the hair I'd long neglected. When he was finished, he turned me toward the mirror. I barely recognized myself. My face, clean-shaven except for a neatly waxed mustache, looked sharper and more deliberate, like someone with a purpose and the means to pursue it. The hair on the sides of my head was clipped close, while the longer hair on top swept like a wave crashing across my forehead.

Other faces materialized behind me in the mirror: those of Marie Laveau and another woman, slender, dressed in orange with a blue tignon.

"This one's going places," said the woman in orange. "Eyes like sapphires in a plate of cream." She pinched my chin. "Baby, you could sell holy water to the Devil."

My face, still burning from the astringent, burned hotter still.

"Now, let's go find you some proper clothes," Jerome said.

I nodded.

I'd put myself in Jerome's hands for a short while with a decent-enough outcome. What harm could a little longer do?

13

Dear Father,

I hope this letter finds you well. I write to inform you that I have fulfilled my lifelong dream of becoming a doctor with my own practice. Yet it is with a heavy heart that I reach this milestone without Mary Beth at my side.

It is with a heavy heart too that I report this success only to you, and not to my mother or sister.

I suppose you take no pleasure in that. Or do you? Isn't that your greatest joy, proving your faith to your God through your treachery to your own family, who actually did exist, and placed their faith in you?

Your loving son,

Hiram

I crumpled the stamped envelope containing the letter and tossed it into the post office trash bin.

The bullet was lodged deep in the man's thigh, and infection had already set in. The duel had taken place two days earlier. With no available beds at Charity, and all the other hospitals shuttered, his family had attempted to extract the bullet themselves, only making matters worse.

"Try Dufilho," a neighbor told the man's frantic wife. "On Chartres Street."

And so here he was: Phineas Jasper, our first real patient, teetering on the precipice between life and death.

Jerome and I tied him to a cot and carried him upstairs. His family tried to follow, but we insisted they wait downstairs. In the operating room, Jerome strapped Jasper to the table while I prepared the ether. The acrid fumes filled the air as I pressed the glass spouts to Jasper's mouth and nostrils. Within moments he was asleep.

We cut away his trousers to reveal a mass of blood-soaked bandages clinging to his thigh. I unwound the filthy strips, exposing raw, inflamed flesh, swollen, discolored, and streaked with pus. The jagged tear at the wound's center spoke to his family's desperate, failed attempts to dig out the bullet.

"Scalpel," I said.

Jerome handed me the instrument, and I cut away the dead, discolored tissue, exposing layers of clotted blood and inflamed flesh.

"Grease," I said.

Jerome slid me the tub of lard. I scooped out a fingerful and probed the wound, Jasper's ample layers of fat and muscle making it difficult to locate the bullet. After several minutes, I pulled my finger out with a wet squelch and wiped my forehead on my sleeve.

"I can't find it," I said. "Could you give it a try?"

Jerome nodded, and I stepped aside. He greased a finger and inserted it into the wound.

"There's the bone," he said, feeling his way along. "Damn, it's really lodged in there." He withdrew his finger and tapped a spot several inches below the opening. "Here." He went to a drawer and retrieved a pair of forceps. "Try these. You might get lucky. Or you might make it worse, and we'll have to drill another hole."

Suddenly, a dark surge of blood pulsed from the wound. We quickly tightened the tourniquet on his upper thigh and the bleeding slowed to a sluggish ooze.

"We need to get it out fast and stitch him up," I said. "You know where it is—can you try again?"

Jerome slid the ether jar toward me. "Brace his knee, in case he convulses."

"Right." I placed one hand on Jasper's knee and the other on the ether jar.

Jerome inserted the forceps into the wound, adjusting the angle as he fished for the bullet.

"There it is," he said. He tried hard to grip it, but it slipped free. "Come on, Jerome," he muttered to himself.

"Should I—"

"I almost had it." He probed again. "Ah, got it."

Jasper gasped. His eyes popped open and his leg jerked so violently I couldn't hold it down.

"Damn it," Jerome said. "I lost it."

I pressed the ether spouts to Jasper's nostrils and lips. "Breathe, Mr. Jasper."

Soon, he slipped back under.

"Sorry," I said.

Jerome shook his head and went back to work. "There it is. Hold him still this time."

"I'm trying to."

Jerome twisted the forceps. "It's really lodged in there." He yanked, then twisted again. "I can feel it slipping." He paused and sighed. "We're going to have to cut that new hole, Doc. It's not coming out."

"Let me try."

"Have at it." He stepped aside.

I gripped the forceps, twisted hard, and the bullet popped free. Blood trickled down Jasper's thigh as I held up the misshapen chunk of metal. Jerome and I exchanged a satisfied look.

"Good job, King Arthur," he said.

After taking a moment to clean ourselves, we prepared to close the wound. I reached for the sugar of lead.

"Don't put that stuff in there, Doc."

It took me aback—not so much the challenge to my authority, but the confidence in his ignorance.

"He'll get gangrene if I don't," I replied.

"He'll get gangrene if you do."

Where did such mistaken beliefs come from? Hadn't Dr. Dufilho taught Jerome anything in all their years together?

"That isn't true," I said, uncorking the vial.

Jerome shook his head. "Any healthy tissue he's got left in there, you'll kill it with that stuff. He'll rot from the inside out, like a tomato in the sun."

"If we don't stimulate the humors with lead," I said, doing my best to control my tone, "his phlegm and red bile will stagnate. Infection and death will follow. Jasper is a man, not a tomato."

Jerome shook his head. "You put that in there, it'll kill him before the bone has a chance to heal. Pack it with honey paste."

I dumped the powder into the wound.

Jerome glared at me. "You did a good thing, Doc, getting that bullet out. Now you just undid the good thing you did. I wouldn't say that if I didn't know what that stuff does to bones."

I didn't want to fight with him. I was already drained from the effort of removing the bullet. I willed myself to stay calm before I spoke. "Have you read the *United States Pharmacopeia*, revised edition, 1830?"

He shook his head.

"Then perhaps *The Principles and Practice of Surgery*, by William Pirrie, published just last year?"

He shook his head again.

"Those texts are the preeminent authorities on the topic. I've read them twice, forward and backward. Nowhere in them does it recommend honey paste, orris root, tonka beans, or Git-You-a-Man powder. The correct, medically prescribed treatment is lead acetate. That is all there is to it. This is a medical establishment, and we will follow proper, proven medical methodology."

Jerome's lips parted, but he remained silent.

Jasper stirred, beginning to wake.

André Boudreaux was the first respondent to our help-wanted notice. He was a slender man with a sallow complexion that hinted at poor health. He met Jerome and me at the apothecary counter and handed over a letter of reference, which we skimmed.

Jerome began the interview. "It says you assisted a Doctor LeBlanc?"

"Oui," Boudreaux replied.

Switching to French, Jerome asked, *"Quelles étaient vos responsabilités là-bas?"*

"Bien, j'ai effectué de nombreuses tâches: l'accueil, le classement, un peu de comptabilité."

Jerome turned to me. "He says he performed many tasks. Reception, filing, some accounting."

I nodded. "And what can you tell us about your medical knowledge, Mr. Boudreaux? Procedures, anatomy, medicines, that sort of thing?"

"Oh, *m'afraid je n'ai pas trop d'expérience dans ce domaine. Juste les responsabilités administratives, vous voyez."*

"He says he doesn't have much medical experience," Jerome translated. "Just administrative work."

A trickle of blood began to leak from Boudreaux's left nostril, which he didn't seem to notice. I tapped Jerome's arm and nodded toward Boudreaux.

"Pardon, monsieur?" Jerome said. *"Vous avez un peu de... fuite ici."*

Boudreaux blinked and swiped at his nose, then frowned at the bright crimson glistening on his fingertips. *"Je dois m'être gratté."*

"He says he must have scratched—" Jerome began, but stopped as a thin rivulet of blood seeped from the corner of Boudreaux's left eye.

As we stared, transfixed, Boudreaux swiped at his face again, smearing blood across his cheek with his hand.

"Je... je dois avoir attrapé un rhume, c'est tout. Juste un petit mal de tête, je crois."

Jerome handed him a towel to stem the flow. "He says it's just a cold, a headache."

I shook my head. This man was in the grip of yellow fever and in no condition for employment—least of all in an apothecary. Worse still, the fever was thought to be contagious, and here he sat, breathing on us, speckling the air with droplets of his infected blood.

"Je pense que ça suffira pour aujourd'hui, monsieur," Jerome said. "I told him that would be all for today."

Boudreaux opened his mouth to protest, but thought better of it. With a nod, he rose unsteadily and stumbled out the door, leaving a trail of scarlet droplets in his wake.

As the door swung shut behind him, I let out a weary sigh, and Jerome shook his head.

Some hours later, the next candidate arrived, a short, buxom woman with hazel eyes, cute freckled nose, and chin-length auburn hair glued by sweat to her apple cheeks. A bone-colored bodice showed at her collar beneath a faded pink blouse. Arriving accompanied by a pungent cloud of lilac, she settled into the chair with a sniffle.

"Candy LaCroix," she announced with an American twang, handing Jerome her calling card.

"Miss LaCroix," we replied.

"Pleasure to meet you handsome fellas," she said, glancing between us. "Two's company, three's a *ménage à trois,* ain't that right?"

Before either of us could respond, Miss LaCroix let out a loud, wet sneeze. "Ugh, 'scuse me." She wiped her nose with the back of her hand. "Allergies acting up something fierce today. On account of the pollen—or so they're saying in all the medical journals I read so religiously."

I discreetly pushed my notebook—now speckled with Miss LaCroix's snot—to the side.

"It says here you're a hospitality worker," Jerome said.

"Yes, sir. Greeter and hostess work, mostly. But I do it all. I'm a real quick learner."

Jerome and I glanced at each other.

"As our front counter woman," I said, "you'd be interacting with unwell patients regularly. I'm concerned your congestion—from the pollen—might disrupt their sense of well-being."

She waved a hand dismissively. "It's just a little head cold, Doc. Nothin' to fret over."

Another sneeze shook her frame, and I paused to let her recover. I already sensed she wasn't the right fit for the position and decided to wrap up the interview.

"Yes, well, thank you for your time, Miss LaCroix. We'll be in touch if we need anything further."

She leaned forward. "I'll do whatever you fellas want, anytime you want. Please just give me a job." Her hand landed on Jerome's thigh and slid upward. "Anything. Anytime. As many times as you want. I ain't fragile."

Jerome cleared his throat. "That's a very tempting offer, Mademoiselle LaCroix. But we'd prefer to interview a few more people before making our decision."

The next applicant to enter was a tall, dignified-looking black man with dark eyes that twinkled with intelligence. He appeared to be in his forties, with streaks of gray in his close-cropped hair. His attire was simple but immaculate: a dark wool frock coat buttoned high, a crisp white shirt, and neatly pressed trousers.

"Good day, sirs," he said, shaking our hands with a firm, steady grip. "My name is LeRoy LeRoix." He produced a neatly folded sheet of cream-colored stationery. "My letter of reference."

Impressed by his refined manner, Jerome and I exchanged a glance. I felt a flicker of hope as I took the letter and motioned for LeRoix to sit. Unfolding the paper, I saw it contained only a sentence or two.

"Your letter is rather sparse, Mr. LeRoix," I said. "But that's perfectly fine. Why don't you tell us a bit about yourself and your qualifications?"

He leaned close and spoke quietly, as though he feared someone might be eavesdropping. "Candidly, doctors, I fled here from Baton Rouge last week. I am an escaped slave and I need a place to lay low while I plan my journey north to freedom. I heard you are both good and trustworthy men."

Jerome and I exchanged another glance.

My heart went out to this man, risking everything to escape bondage. Yet I wondered: from whom had he heard such a thing about us?

"That is a remarkable journey, Mr. LeRoix," I said. "But I have reservations about offering you this position, given your... unfortunate circumstances."

LeRoix's face fell, but he nodded. "I understand—you have a business to protect. But perhaps there's something I could do in the back?" He glanced toward the courtyard. "Away from prying eyes?"

Suddenly, the baying of dogs echoed down the street.

LeRoix froze. "I must go, sirs," he said. "Perhaps I'll return later to discuss that position."

Before we could say another word, he sprang from his chair and raced out the door.

Jerome and I sat in stunned silence.

Moments later, two men on horseback galloped past, dogs at their heels, heading the same direction LeRoix had fled.

14

The next morning, half an hour before opening for business, I sat on my third-floor balcony enjoying a cigar and a cup of coffee. I'd bought a bundle of twenty cigars for a dollar, half the rate I'd pay for singles, because I'd noticed they helped curb my appetite for morphine.

Jerome had brewed the coffee, and I had to admit it was even better than the coffee at Café du Petit Coin. Or perhaps it just seemed that way because I was enjoying it on my own balcony, thirty feet above the squalor in the streets below.

I'd just begun reading an article in the *Pelican* about the latest skirmishes in the Indian Wars up in Wyoming, a subject of more than passing interest to me, when a flash of orange caught my eye. I set down the newspaper and stood to watch a black woman in a red-and-yellow dress and orange tignon walking up the street from the direction of the cathedral. It was difficult to make out her face at this distance, but I felt sure she was the same woman who'd called me "Sugar" downstairs in the apothecary a month ago.

As I watched her, she stopped, looked up, smiled, and waved. Any worries I'd had about the day ahead evaporated.

The woman—Charlotte, if I remembered correctly—disappeared beneath the balcony. A moment later, a vigorous knock sounded at the front door.

Assuming she was here to interview for the job, and eager to be in her presence again, I spun toward the balcony door and banged my knee against the table, splashing coffee onto my trousers. I cursed under my breath and stepped inside.

As I reached for clean trousers, Jerome's voice carried up from below. "Hello there, Miss Charlotte. What a nice surprise. Did you come for the job?"

"Good morning, Jerome. What job would that be?"

"The front counter job, Miss Charlotte. We placed a notice in the paper."

"No, honey-baby. I'm here to talk about real estate."

Honey-baby. Surely a notch above Sugar. I felt a twinge of jealousy. I dressed quickly and went downstairs.

In the courtyard, I found Jerome and Charlotte seated by the fountain, where Jerome was flipping through a stack of documents. Charlotte noticed me and smiled. Jerome looked up and frowned.

"Good morning, Miss," I said. "Hiram Whitaker."

Charlotte extended her hand. I took it, bowed slightly, and kissed it.

"Oh my," she said, "I guess there's still one gentleman left in New Orleans. Charlotte France."

"To what do we owe the pleasure—" I began.

"I recognized you up there on the balcony, even without that beard. I saw those pretty blue eyes from halfway down the street and just knew it was the same handsome man I met before."

I didn't know what to say.

"You two've met before?" Jerome said.

"Only in passing," Charlotte replied. "But we'll fix that soon enough." She winked at me.

A rush of heat rose in my chest. Not only did she remember me, she wished to know me better.

"She isn't here for the job," Jerome said.

"Then what—"

"She's here for the house."

"The house?"

"That's right," Charlotte said.

"I'm afraid I don't understand."

"Charlotte is Mr. Dufilho's daughter."

I blinked, trying to register his meaning. "You mean Sarah Dufilho is—"

"*Noire?*" Charlotte said. "*Non, monsieur*—forgive me, what was it?"

"Whitaker. Hiram T. Whitaker."

"Hiram T. Whitaker. A beautiful, musical name. Like a pair of George Frederick Bristow's triplets, *n'est-ce pas?* Hiram-T, Whi-ta-ker. *Mais non,* Monsieur Whitaker, my mother was Stella France."

"Ah," I replied, though I had no idea who that was.

"Stella was Mr. Dufilho's housekeeper," Jerome said. "Before he married Patience."

"My mother was Monsieur Dufilho's *placée*," Charlotte said.

"*Placée?*"

"It means he 'placed' her," Jerome explained. "In an apartment on Rampart Street, across from Congo Square."

"They were lovers, Monsieur Whitaker. Sarah lost interest in romance after giving birth to their third child. But my father was still a young man, barely forty. Naturally, he began an affair. When Sarah caught them—right here," she said, gesturing toward Jerome's quarters, "she demanded he fire my mother."

Jerome shrugged. "Paid me a little extra to get lost when they needed privacy."

"It would have been difficult for my mother to find work elsewhere. And my father Louis couldn't bear the thought of my mother under another man's roof. So he rented the apartment on *rue du Rempart* for her and promised to take care of her and their child—*c'est moi*—for the rest of our lives."

She smiled, as if this arrangement were the most natural thing in the world.

I sighed.

"C'est normal," Charlotte said.

"It doesn't sound *normal* to me," I replied.

"There are hundreds of *placées* on Rampart Street," Jerome said.

I rubbed the back of my skull, which had begun to throb. "But what's this about the house? Which house do you mean? The one on Rampart Street?"

Jerome shook his head.

"Non, Monsieur," Charlotte said. "I mean this house."

"I still don't understand."

Jerome handed me the documents and I glanced through them. There was something about 514 Chartres Street, Property of Louis J. Dufilho, Event of Death... one half to ex-wife Sarah and her children, a quarter to Patience, and a quarter to Stella France or her heirs.

I looked up. "But why are you here instead of your mother?"

"My mother is dead, Monsieur Whitaker. I am her heir. As he promised, my father took care of me—paid my rent and sent me a small sum each month. I made ends meet with my little herb shop. But now that my father has passed away, I can't afford to rent either the apartment or the shop. That's why this house must be sold: so I can claim my share of the inheritance."

I flipped to the last page, where the signatures of Louis Dufilho, his lawyer, and a notary confirmed the document's authenticity.

"Is this the only copy of this document?"

Charlotte laughed. "Of course not, Monsieur Whitaker. I'm not *stupide*. There are two more copies, kept by men who have my best interest at heart."

"I see."

I explained my lease arrangement with Patience Dufilho, and then said, "It seems neither she nor Sarah knows about your mother's share. When you submit your claim, their lawyers will contest it. It might take years to settle."

"That's true," Jerome said, nodding.

"And I've only just started my practice," I added. "Mrs. Dufilho promised me just six months. But now, with legal wrangling over claims, percentages, escrow, and so forth, we may have more time. With both wives living in New York, correspondence alone could take weeks, if not months."

"I cannot wait that long, monsieur. I've already been evicted from my apartment, and I'm on the verge of losing my shop."

"Where are you staying?" Jerome asked.

"At Victor Vilberg's house."

"Oh, boy."

"It's only temporary."

"You're not—?"

"Prostituting myself? Don't be absurd, Jerome."

I paced for a moment.

"Why don't you stay here?" I said. "There's a room on the third floor, Bethany's old room. You could work here, too. We need someone at the front counter. I can't pay you yet, but I'll be able to soon. You could continue running your herb shop during your off-hours, if you like."

She frowned but seemed to consider it.

"Well, what do you say, Miss Charlotte?" Jerome said. "It seems like a fair offer."

Charlotte smiled. "I say I will accept."

I clapped my hands together.

"On one condition," she said.

"Condition, Miss Charlotte?" Jerome asked.

"I will take my father's bedroom," she said, turning to me. "And you, Monsieur Whitaker, will take Bethany's."

15

Mrs. Gloria Stenman, a compact, robustly built woman in her forties, was the first patient on our second day of business. She arrived accompanied by her husband Oral, a man of similar stature. Mr. Stenman informed us his wife had come for her regular appointment with Dr. Dufilho. After explaining that he had passed away and that I had taken over his practice, I invited them to sit in the waiting area to discuss Mrs. Stenman's medical needs.

"Mrs. Stenman is here for her monthly treatment," Mr. Stenman said.

"Doctor Dufilho's patient records are upstairs," I explained. "I haven't yet had the chance to review them thoroughly. Perhaps you could tell me, what exactly was Mrs. Stenman's monthly treatment?"

"Mrs. Stenman," he said, taking his wife's hand, "comes here for her monthly rectal dilation."

"Rectal dilation," I repeated, doing my best to maintain a professional demeanor.

It wasn't the sort of procedure I'd hoped to start my day with. Moreover, I'd only skimmed the few pages devoted to the topic in *Gunn's Domestic Medicine* and hadn't had the opportunity to practice it at Saint Anne's.

"Mrs. Stenman is up to size four now," Mr. Stenman said, with obvious pride.

"And this is to treat her...?"

"Lady troubles," he replied.

"Perhaps I should review your wife's records. Or, if you know the precise condition? I'd like to ensure she's receiving the proper treatment."

"Constipation, I believe."

I glanced at Mrs. Stenman, who nodded almost imperceptibly.

"Ah, well," I said, "Then I'd recommend castor oil, three times daily—"

"The occasional hemorrhoid," Mr. Stenman added.

"In that case, we could prescribe calomel."

"A touch of rectal prolapse," he added to the list.

"Rectal prolapse," I repeated.

"On account of her loose pelvic floor, Doctor Dufilho says. Seven kids in eleven years, you know."

I nodded. "Yes, that could certainly cause significant strain to the, uh..."

"The missus suffers a lot in life, Doc. If you can't do her monthly treatment like Doctor Dufilho did, then I know plenty others in town who'd be happy to."

"If I could just check upstairs to see if the dilators are still available?"

"We'll wait right here," Mr. Stenman said, patting his wife's knee.

Jerome, who had been arranging items in the display case, stood and said, "There's a box upstairs by the counter, Doc. Says Lady Troubles right on it."

"Could you show me, Jerome? One moment, Mr. and Mrs. Stenman."

Jerome and I went upstairs. From the box labeled *Lady Troubles* he retrieved a leather bag holding four dilators made of smooth, black rubber, numbered 1 through 4. The size of the Number 4 struck me as disturbingly large for its intended purpose.

"Have you assisted with this treatment before, Jerome?"

"Once or twice."

"I assume Doctor Dufilho used some sort of lubricant?"

"Here you go." He handed me a metal canister labeled Young's Rectal Lubricant.

I read the label aloud: "For her comfort, rendering the canal soft, supple, and pliable while removing all trace of pain and discomfort. Made from only the finest beef tallow and laudanum."

I unscrewed the lid and took a cautious sniff. The mixture of rancid fat and cloyingly sweet medicine produced an odor that made me gag. I quickly resealed the canister.

"What can you tell me about Doctor Dufilho's, er, method?"

Jerome guided Mrs. Stenman behind the modesty screen while I made sure the examination table was properly prepared. When they emerged, Mrs. Stenman wore a long white gown.

Jerome helped her onto the table and gently positioned her. "Just lie on your side as usual, ma'am. You're in good hands with Doctor Whitaker. Lady troubles happens to be his specialty."

He winked at me.

I adjusted the pillow beneath her head. "Are you comfortable, Mrs. Stenman?"

"Yes, somewhat."

"Your husband mentioned you've been suffering from constipation?"

"Sometimes. Occasionally."

"And how long has it been since you've gone?"

"Some days."

"I see. And after this treatment, how soon are you usually able to go?"

"Straight away, sometimes. When the treatment hits the spot, you know."

"Straight away, meaning...?"

"Not right here, of course. I can usually make it to the chamber pot."

Jerome nodded discreetly toward the porcelain bedpan on the shelf.

"Well, then, let's proceed, Mrs. Stenman."

"I'm ready."

I slid the hem of her gown up to her hips. "Still comfortable, ma'am?"

"Comfortable enough."

"Good, good."

"Just..."

"Yes, Mrs. Stenman?"

"I'd prefer we do it alone this time. Without this... colored person intruding on us."

"I assure you, ma'am, Jerome's presence is essential for this procedure. I understand he's assisted with it many times before."

"But this time I'd prefer it just be me and you. For my privacy. I don't care to be seen, you know, down there, by colored people."

Jerome spoke up. "There are some things I need to take care of downstairs, Doc. Come get me if you need anything." He tapped the canister of lubricant on his way out.

"You say you were up to the Number 3?"

"Doctor Dufilho said we should use the Number 4, if I wished to get the most benefit."

"Your benefit is my only concern, Mrs. Stenman. Let's try the Number 4, shall we?"

I dipped two fingers into the canister and scooped out a dollop. With as steady a hand as I could muster, I applied the lubricant to the area in question.

"Be sure to use the Number 4," Mrs. Stenman said.

"I've got it right here, Mrs. Stenman. All right, here we go." I inserted the tip. "How does that feel? Comfortable?"

"Deeper," she replied. "I can't feel it."

"I think you shouldn't, Mrs. Stenman. The lubricant is meant to numb you, and I don't wish—"

"I need to feel something."

"Right." I pushed the instrument deeper, then paused.

After a moment, she wiggled her hips. "If you don't stimulate it, nothing will happen. That's what Doctor Dufilho said."

I commenced easing the device in and out, as Jerome had instructed.

"Doctor Dufilho put his other hand in front, for support."

"In front?"

"Yes. In front."

If ever Mary Beth was going to check in on me from the spirit realm, now would be the time. Yet, I couldn't refuse this patient's request for care. If Dr. Dufilho, a far more seasoned physician than I, had approved of this treatment, then—

She wiggled her bottom again. "Hand in front," she said. "For support."

I hesitated, considering the angles of approach: between the thighs or around the hip.

"Give me your hand," she said.

Around the hip, then.

She guided my hand to her lower abdomen. I could see what she meant: it did provide support against the thrusting action of the Number 4.

In and out, in and out, as her body rocked gently to and fro.

Trade was slow at first, though we did do steady business in quinine, castor oil, camphor ointment, turpentine, and other common remedies. Glycerin, sulfur, and ipecac were also in demand. Longtime customers were pleased that most of Dr. Dufilho's offerings were still available at Whitaker's Apothecary. And when they requested items I no longer carried—typically those of dubious medicinal value—they were generally satisfied with the more authentic alternatives I provided.

Three days after Mrs. Stenman's procedure, her husband Oral came in alone. He reported that the treatment had been a success and that Mrs. Stenman's mood was greatly improved. He shook my hand and said, "Anyone asks me or the missus for a recommendation, they'll hear about Doctor Whitaker's, count on my word."

"Thank you, Mr. Stenman. Her constipation has resolved, then?"

"Constipation? Oh, yes, no mention of it."

Charlotte moved in and began her employment. Her arrival proved timely, as the next few days were busy ones for Jerome and me. The first day began with the extraction of a rotten molar. Jerome held the patient, Mr. Hunnicutt, steady as I tugged at the blackened stump. Instead of coming out cleanly, the tooth crumbled, releasing a stench that made us recoil. I removed the remaining shards and prepared to pack the cavity with a lard-based paste of arsenic and turpentine.

"Beeswax and witch hazel," Jerome whispered, once we were out of Hunnicutt's earshot. "If you want that hole to heal up."

I shook my head. "We'll use the accepted medical treatments. And we will do so without fail."

* * *

Later that day, Mr. Jasper, the man from whose thigh we had extracted the bullet, was brought in by his wife and children, complaining of severe pain. Jerome and I helped him upstairs and strapped him to the operating table. I administered fifteen milligrams of morphine by injection. Once he ceased writhing, we began removing the blood-soaked bandages. The reek that hit us was unbearable, driving us out onto the balcony for air. If I'd believed nothing could compare to Mr. Hunnicutt's disintegrated molar, I was sorely mistaken. When we returned and finished unwrapping Mr. Jasper's bandages, we were confronted with a sight more horrific than anything I'd witnessed during my residency at Saint Anne's. His thigh was grotesquely swollen, the area around the wound caved in and weeping thick, yellow-green pus. The blackening muscle was streaked yellow and blue. Marrow oozed from the exposed bone, which was yellowed and decayed. Jerome and I exchanged a grim look.

I felt sick to my stomach. Amputations were the most horrifying procedures I'd ever performed. Yet I tried to project an outward calm.

"You want me to do this one, Doc?"

"I'll do it. Prepare the ether and bring me the scalpels."

"What are you doing?" Jasper croaked.

"We're going to save your life, Mr. Jasper. But in order to do that, we must amputate your leg. It's become infected, and I'm afraid it can't be saved."

"What? No! Get Myrtle. Get me out of here!"

Jerome returned with the ether jar ready. "We should get the wife's written permission, or we'll get sued. That's what Mr. Dufilho always said. Can't sew the leg back on if he's unhappy with the results." He turned away from Mr. Jasper and mouthed, *or if he dies.*

I nodded. "Then go downstairs and get her consent, before it's too late."

Jerome disappeared, leaving me alone with Mr. Jasper. I took his hand. It was hot and damp. I poured a glass of water from a pitcher and held it to his parched lips. He shook his head.

"I didn't think I was gonna die," he said. "I thought I got lucky. I didn't want that duel. I don't even know what we was fightin' about."

"You did get lucky, Mr. Jasper. You're alive. And now you're going to keep on living."

Jerome returned. "She signed the papers."

"You do want to live, don't you, Mr. Jasper?" I asked.

He gave a faint nod.

"Then you will. Jerome, apply the ether."

Jerome held the glass tubes to Jasper's nose and mouth. His breathing slowed, his limbs slackened, and his eyes fluttered shut.

I took the scalpel and sliced away the dead skin and flesh, cutting a clean margin below which I would saw through the bone. Jerome collected the discarded tissue into a bucket. Despite the tourniquet, each time I severed a major vessel, blood sprayed out before Jerome could clamp it, coating our aprons and splattering our arms and faces. Soon, we were drenched in Mr. Jasper's blood. After removing the necrotic tissue and preparing the upper area for suturing, I took the saw and positioned it against the leg. I drew the blade back, then pushed it forward. Back, forward. To and fro.

It took less than three minutes to saw through the bone, after which the leg dropped to the floor with a dull thump. I could scarcely imagine a farewell more final, and felt as if I had lost something, too. What would become of that leg? I wondered, as I struggled to maintain control of my emotions. The municipal waste collectors had long since ceased their rounds. Jerome would do something with it, I supposed. Someday I might ask him about it.

Turning away from the lonely appendage on the floor, I commenced cleaning and bandaging the stump. When I reached for the sugar of lead, Jerome and I exchanged a glance, but neither of us said a word.

Over the next few days, I visited Mr. Jasper's home several times, determined to ensure his survival. I changed his bandages, applied mercuric ointment, administered morphine injections and liquid opium, treated his fever with quinine, and re-stitched the flaps on his stump. On the fourth day, his fever broke, and I left his house with a sense of cautious optimism. I returned to Whitaker's Apothecary to find Jerome sprinting out the front door and down the banquette.

"Jerome!" I called after him, "Where are you going?"

He didn't stop, didn't even look back. Just vanished around the corner, leaving me standing there, bewildered.

16

I stepped into the apothecary to find a young white woman in a blue-and-white dress speaking with Charlotte at the front counter. Noticing me, they fell silent.

"What's going on?" I asked. "Where did Jerome run off to?"

"Doctor Whitaker, this is Veronica McFarland," Charlotte said. "Jerome does her hair."

McFarland? This couldn't be good.

"A pleasure to meet you, Miss McFarland," I said.

She nodded glumly.

"Arabella's run off again," Charlotte said.

"Run off?"

"Third or fourth time she's tried to escape."

"Escape?"

"Veronica's uncle owns her."

"Your uncle is J.W. McFarland?"

"Yes, sir. He'll catch her. He always does. She's a fool to keep running."

"Beats her nearly to death every time," Charlotte said. "But that doesn't stop her."

"He swore the last time he'd finish the job if she ever ran again," Veronica said. "Those were his exact words."

"He didn't mean it, I'm sure," I said.

They exchanged a glance.

"He tries not to kill the pregnant ones," Veronica said. "But he intends to make an example of her this time. She's run away too many times. It disturbs the order among the other slaves."

"Is that what you told Jerome? That he intends to make an example of her?"

Veronica nodded. "He had a right to know."

"Do either of you know where she might have gone? Or where Jerome might have gone to look for her?"

Veronica shook her head.

"No idea," Charlotte said.

"They caught her one time in the swamp," Veronica said. "That's all I know."

Before I could say more, a black man burst through the door, cradling a young girl in his arms.

"You gotta help her!" he cried.

The girl's mother followed close behind, with red eyes and a face streaked with tears.

"Yes, of course," I said.

"There's no room at Charity, nowhere else to go," the man said.

"I have to be going," Veronica muttered, easing backward toward the door.

"Let's get this child upstairs," I said.

"If you need help, I can—" Charlotte began.

"I'll take care of her," I replied. "Stay here and mind the apothecary."

I led the family upstairs and directed the father to lay his daughter on the table. I began a quick examination with the father hovering nearby while the mother slumped into a chair by the balcony doors and wept. The girl's skin was tinged yellow, and beads of sweat glistened on her cheeks, though her body was cold to the touch. Her pulse fluttered faintly and her breathing was shallow and labored. Her abdomen was swollen and taut. Dark, purplish splotches mottled her legs—signs her blood had already begun to corrupt.

I had to save this girl.

I considered the usual treatments—bleeding and purgatives to balance the humors, sedating with laudanum—but they struck me as too harsh for someone so small and frail. I doubted whether she could survive the disease or the cure.

"Doc? What are you doing? You gotta do something," the father pleaded. "You gotta help her!"

I rested my palm on the girl's forehead. It was colder now, damp and clammy. I moved aside a tangle of curls and opened one eyelid. The eyeball had rolled back and the white was tinged a sickly yellowish orange.

"Doc! Do something!" her father cried again. "Please!"

The mother's sobs rose, filling the room.

Charlotte appeared beside me with a damp towel and wiped the sweat from the girl's brow.

"Get more wet cloths," she said. "We have to cool her down."

She moved quickly, wiping the girl's face, neck, chest, and limbs. I fetched more towels and soaked them in cold water.

"Come on, baby. You got to live," Charlotte said. She leaned in and pressed her head against the girl's chest.

"You a nurse?" the man asked.

"Yes," I said, before she could answer. "She's my nurse."

Charlotte shot me a glance, then resumed her work. After a moment, she lifted her head. "Keep wetting her down. I'll be right back."

She returned shortly with two sachets and handed me one. "Mix that in water," she said.

I emptied the package into a glass and stirred. "What is it?" I whispered.

"Lavender and echinacea root," she whispered back. "To cool her down."

"And what are you rubbing on her chest?"

"Catnip. Helps break the fever."

The girl's mother clasped her hands in silent prayer and pressed them to her lips. Tears streamed down her face. "God, please, save her," she whispered.

Charlotte gently tilted the girl's head back and fed her small sips of lavender water. She resumed rubbing the catnip salve across her chest and stomach, whispering a prayer:

"God, Good Guide, Great Master Spirits, bless this beloved lavender steeped in cool waters. Lower the fires of suffering, bind Satan's grip, grant the grace of the Good Mother. Let this remedy breathe life into this child and send the fever away. Protect this lamb of God. Amen."

"Amen," the mother and father echoed, their voices full of fragile hope.

Suddenly, the girl groaned. Her eyes fluttered open. She smiled faintly at her father, lifted her head, then coughed up a gob of black bile that landed on my arm. Her head dropped back onto the table. The light faded from her eyes.

A crushing silence descended.

The father's expression twisted in disbelief. "Baby? Danielle? Baby!"

The mother rushed to the table. Her trembling hands cupped her daughter's face. When she saw what had happened, she threw her head back and wailed in agonized grief.

My knees buckled, and I grabbed the edge of the table.

I fell ill and stayed in bed for several days, fearing I'd caught the fever from the dying girl. With Jerome still gone, I relied on Charlotte to treat me with morphine and quinine. For the first two days, neither of us spoke about Danielle. But on the third morning, after checking in on me, and before going downstairs to open the apothecary, Charlotte paused in the doorway and we held each other's gaze.

"There wasn't anything you could've done for her," she said.

I didn't know whether that was true or not, but I lacked the energy to argue. "I know."

"Sometimes, they're too far along. On that road."

I nodded.

"Nothing I could have done, either," she said.

I propped myself up. "Then why did you try? Why rub her in catnip and invoke those voodoo spells?"

She shook her head and turned to leave, but hesitated, her hand resting on the doorframe. She turned back. "To make them feel better. To ease their hurt."

I nodded again.

"You know what, Doctor Whitaker?"

I waited.

"You can't make anyone live forever. Sometimes all you can do is make it hurt a little bit less. But that's a lot."

I reached for the cup of lemongrass tea she'd brought me in lieu of the laudanum I'd asked for.

"Here's what you don't understand," she said. "They knew she was going to die. You could see it in their eyes. But they couldn't bear that kind of pain. All they could do was hope to ease her suffering; and they needed someone to ease theirs, too."

I set down the tea. "Thank you, Charlotte."

When she didn't move from the door, I added, "Sincerely."

She nodded and turned away, and I listened to the sound of her footsteps descending the stairwell until it faded into silence.

Later, a knock roused me from a fitful slumber.

"Yes?" I called, my voice hoarse.

Charlotte opened the door and leaned in. "McFarland's downstairs. He wants to talk to you."

"Tell him I'm sick."

"I did. He said it's urgent, and for you to pull yourself together and get out of bed."

"Rather high rate of failure, wouldn't you agree?" McFarland said, tossing a folder of medical records onto the counter. He tapped the topmost one—Danielle Johnson's.

"Charity lost six-hundred and twenty-four to the fever last week," I replied, trying to keep my voice steady, and to avoid coughing in McFarland's face.

"None of them blacks, of course," he said. "Oh, but I should give you the benefit of the doubt: the Johnsons were free, after all. None of the health benefits of slavery."

He flipped aside Danielle's page, revealing the Jasper file.

"This one, though. Run-of-the-mill bullet extraction. Yet the poor fellow loses a leg. Outcomes like that don't reflect well on you or the profession as a whole. Not really up to the Medical Board's standards, wouldn't you agree?"

"The bullet was lodged deeply into his femur. We did the best we could under the circumstances."

He shook his head, glanced at the report again, then tapped one of the entries. "Only two grams lead acetate, I see. Had it been three, your man Jasper might still have two legs."

"Two grams is the maximum dose prescribed by the 1830 *United States Pharmacopeia, revised edition.* Any more could prove toxic."

"This isn't 1830, Whicket. It's 1853. Perhaps if you kept up with the latest science, you'd know three grams is the recommended dosage for amputations." He pushed the file aside. "But that's not why I'm here. I take it you're aware that your boy Jerome is kin to one of my slaves—Arabella. She's run off again, and I need a word with him."

"I haven't seen him for several days; I have no idea where he's gone."

He raised an eyebrow. "You don't know the whereabouts of your own slave?"

"He's free to come and go as he pleases."

"It won't look good for you if your boy's aiding and abetting a runaway. He isn't free to do as he pleases if it abets a crime. And trust me, the authorities will hold you accountable for his actions."

"But as I was saying—"

"The punishment for aiding and abetting is the same as running away."

"I don't really keep up with the—"

"Sixty lashes or death. Whichever comes first. My money's usually on death."

Struggling to keep my composure, I said, "It's not really the decent way to treat another human being, is it?"

"For the love of God, Whicket! Neither is sawing off a perfectly good leg. But we do what we must for the greater good. Surely you'd agree to that much?"

I sighed. "What I'd agree to is that—"

"Ephesians, Whicket," he said, raising a clenched fist. "'Slaves, obey your earthly masters with fear and trembling, as you obey Christ.'"

"I don't think Ephesians—"

McFarland held up his hand to silence me, then smoothed his coat and straightened his cuffs.

"When your boy shows up, remind him there's no place for him—or his kin—to run to. If he's aiding Arabella, he might as well dig his own grave."

I had grown terribly lonely during my months at Saint Anne's. Even surrounded by coworkers and treating dozens of patients a day, I had cut myself off from any real human connection, even with Emma, the closest thing I had to a friend. But by the time I was ready to move beyond the grief that had followed me to New Orleans, it was too late.

Everyone was gone. And now, just as I'd found something like friendship with Jerome, he too was gone. Just as Emma, Mary Beth, my sister, and my mother were all gone.

But Charlotte remained. Strong, beautiful, charming, funny Charlotte. How long, I wondered, before she too would be gone? While organizing medicines in the display cases or on the shelves, I found myself straining to hear her interactions with customers, listening to her charm them as easily as she charmed me. More than a few people, men and women both, returned to buy things they claimed to have forgotten: earwax spoon, tongue scraper, corn salve—just to linger a moment longer in her presence or chat with her for another minute or two, before leaving with a lighter step. At closing time, we'd speak briefly—about Jerome and Arabella, the day's business, the patients we'd seen, bits of gossip she'd heard, ideas she had for the apothecary. Then she'd leave for the herb shop, and a familiar gloom would settle over me. The house would feel too large, the rooms too empty, the silence deafening. I'd retreat to my study, bury myself in medical texts until the light faded, then sit out on the balcony, smoking a cigar and drinking tea, searching the street for a familiar face. Jerome's, Emma's, especially Charlotte's.

But she never returned home before I went to sleep.

And was it really home? For her? For me? For anyone? It had been Jerome's once; would it be again?

I'd lie awake in bed for hours, my thoughts circling in endless worry.

And then, five days after he'd run off, Jerome came home.

17

Jerome had searched everywhere Arabella might have gone. He didn't share the details, and I didn't press him. But McFarland's men found her first, in a house only a few streets over from his townhouse in the American Quarter.

"She was hiding with the Inner Light people," Jerome told Charlotte and me as we sat in the courtyard together. "Even I didn't know about that place."

"Inner Light?" I asked.

"Quakers. Levi and Greta Woolman. Turns out they ran an Underground Railroad station out of their home. He's a dentist, shes a teacher. Now they're outlaws, on the run."

Someone had tipped off McFarland's men, who broke down the Woolmans' door in the middle of the night. They found three slaves there, including Arabella, eight months pregnant. Jerome guessed the Woolmans had been escorting other slaves to the next station when it happened.

The other two submitted to McFarland's men, but Arabella fought back despite her condition, cutting one man's arm to the bone. He lunged for her throat before the others restrained him—she was McFarland's prized property, after all, and the baby inside her was worth a pretty penny.

"She told me she wanted to die rather than give birth to another slave," Jerome said. "She tried to provoke that man to kill her."

Charlotte shook her head. "She doesn't have to die if she doesn't want to have that baby. She ought to know that."

"She knows about pennyroyal," Jerome replied. "But she said she wouldn't murder her own child."

We fell silent, trying to make sense of it.

"She'd rather die with a baby in her womb than use pennyroyal?" I said.

"She's confused," Charlotte said.

"She believes it's a sin," Jerome said. "She's a Christian. She doesn't want to go to hell."

My thoughts turned to McFarland and his cold, shriveled heart. How, I asked myself, could I have staked my future on the whims of such a monstrous creature?

A few nights later, I stayed up late, hoping to catch sight of Charlotte returning from her herb shop. Midnight came and went without any sign of her.

I stepped onto the balcony and scanned the street below, faintly illuminated here and there by flickering gas lamps. The night was stifling, the air was thick and teeming with mosquitoes. Frustrated, I withdrew inside, extinguished the lamp, and lay down to sleep.

I woke abruptly to the sharp, maddening buzz of a mosquito near my ear. I swatted at it, only to feel its bite. Groggy and irritated, I stumbled out of bed, poured water from the pitcher into my hand, and splashed it into my ear.

The buzzing ceased, but I remained uneasy, afraid the mosquito might still be trapped inside my ear.

I poured a glass of water, hoping it would calm my nerves, and wandered back to the balcony. I checked my pocket watch—2:47.

Footsteps.

I leaned over the railing and peered down at two figures approaching along the banquette. As they passed beneath a gas lamp, the amber glow revealed their identities: Charlotte, her hair wrapped in an orange tignon; and a tall, dark-skinned man dressed impeccably in a black suit and top hat.

They were holding hands.

There was something familiar about the man, but I couldn't place him.

I stepped back, my pulse quickening.

Hearing the clink of the front door opening and closing, I hurried inside and pressed my ear to my bedroom door, straining to catch their voices as they floated up the stairwell.

"Your house is magnificent, Charlotte darling," the man said.

"Wait until you see my bedroom," Charlotte replied.

A door clicked shut.

I moved quietly to the balcony.

"Doctor Whitaker, up so late?" said a familiar voice.

Startled, I turned to find Charlotte and her guest already on the adjacent balcony. The man doffed his top hat, revealing tight black curls glinting with pomade on one side, and on the other a bare skullcap of skin: syphilitic alopecia, I thought, or maybe scalp ringworm. His eyes appeared momentarily to flash from within, though it might only have been the reflection of some distant lamplight.

"Allow me to introduce Baron Sunday," Charlotte said, smiling easily, as if there were nothing unusual about her bringing a man home, and at this hour.

I remembered the name from Antoinette's dream but didn't know what to make of it.

"Pleasure to meet you, Mr. Sunday," I said.

"Pleasure's entirely mine, Monsieur le docteur," he replied.

I glanced between them, trying to grasp the nature of their relationship, as Charlotte's perfume—sandalwood and jasmine—drifted across the space between us.

"Baron of what sort, exactly?" I asked.

He smiled, revealing teeth that were long and crooked but preternaturally white.

"Astute question, Herr docteur. My parents were from Haiti, but they pursued their doctorates in Paris; Father in Chemistry, Mother in Medicine. Legally possible, mind you, but socially obstructed. Fortunately, they held influence. While abroad, they fell under the spell of royalty. My mother wanted to name me King, but my father prevailed, thank the Good God. Thus, Baron."

"Doctor Whitaker," Charlotte said, "we'll wake the whole neighborhood like this. Come, join us in my room."

"What? No, I don't wish to be a bother—"

"Then I insist. Otherwise, I shall be quite bothered."

I glanced down at my gray flannel pajamas. "Perhaps just for a minute. Let me change into something more—"

"Nonsense, come as you are. And monsieur, don't dawdle. We're dying for you to join us. Isn't that right, Baron?"

"Dying," he confirmed.

A moment later, I stood at her door. It opened before I could knock.

"Why, Doctor Whitaker—what a pleasant surprise," Charlotte said. "Come in, monsieur, come."

The room had changed since I'd last seen it. A mosquito net hung over the four-poster bed. The couchette was covered in a vibrant African-patterned cloth. Bottles and jars crowded the writing desk. On the wall opposite the bed hung a painting of a man who bore a striking resemblance to Mr. Sunday, standing beside an open grave, a bouquet of black-petaled roses dangling from his fingers. I tried to fathom how there could be a painting so similar to Antoinette's dream, but I couldn't come up with anything.

"I found it in the back of the closet," Charlotte said. "I assumed Patience must have left it behind. It's lovely, don't you think?"

Just then, Mr. Sunday entered from the balcony, holding two glasses.

"There you are," he said, handing me one.

The liquid within sparkled in the dim light. I sniffed it —fruity and tangy, with effervescent bubbles that stung my nostrils.

"Bubbling wine from France," he said. "Something this therapeutic might put me out of business. Might put the both of us out of business, now that I think of it."

I accepted the glass. The coolness against my fingers was a relief in the oppressive heat. I took a sip. The flavor and the feeling of it in my mouth were magnificent.

"Not bad," I said.

Turning back to the painting, I noticed the date scrawled in the lower left—1804. I glanced at Mr. Sunday. "Tell me," I said, "have you and Charlotte known each other long?"

"Oh yes, for all time," he replied.

"Forever, it seems," Charlotte added.

She stood close now, close enough that I could feel her breath against my skin, cool and sweet with the tang of the champagne.

"Funny you should mention that," I said to Mr. Sunday. "You bear a striking resemblance to—"

The words caught in my throat.

The painting tilted, dimmed, then blackened, as though smoke had crept across its surface. Then, before my eyes, it faded away.

I awoke at dawn in my bed. The champagne flute stood empty on the nightstand. Beside it lay an empty sachet.

18

September 12, 1853

Dear Father,

We are doing well in our little apothecary and medical practice, receiving new customers every day. New Orleans teems with the sick and the injured, all seeking the curative powers of real medicine and the healing touch of a qualified physician.

As you know, I have dedicated my life to this noble profession and take great pride in the work I do here alongside my esteemed associates, Jerome de La Chance and Charlotte France.

Just yesterday, Jerome and I were called to the bedside of a young man suffering from a persistent cough. After a brief examination, we determined that leeching would be the best course of treatment. I set to work, carefully applying them to his chest.

The procedure didn't go as smoothly as I'd hoped. The leeches were particularly slippery and energetic, and in my haste one latched onto my own wrist and began to draw blood. As I worked to detach it, our patient erupted into a violent coughing fit, spraying mucus and spittle across my face and waistcoat. It was all I could do to maintain my composure and see the treatment through. If I never knew what an adventure medicine could be, I do now.

Charlotte is quite the charmer, and I sometimes suspect people visit our apothecary solely to bask in her presence, much as beachgoers visit the shore to bask in the sunshine and salty air.

Speaking of Charlotte's charms, the other day she found Jerome and me at the front windows, scraping off the gold-leaf lettering that read Dufilho's Pharmacy in preparation for the new name: Whitaker's Apothecary and Medical. She was of the strongly expressed opinion that this name was not merely bad but terrible, lacking the minutest trace of appeal or marketing savoir faire. We don't have apothecaries in New Orleans, she insisted—we have pharmacies. And what could be duller than Medical? It must be, she declared, Healing Arts. It must be Whitaker's Pharmacy & Healing Arts.

I explained, as calmly as I could, that in the North we called them apothecaries. She replied, far less calmly, that here they are called pharmacies. It was the French way, the Creole way. I was neither French nor Creole, I reminded her, nor did I intend to resort to French or Creole quackery. I would use proper Northern medicine, and the name would reflect that: apothecary, not pharmacy.

But as a gesture of peace, I agreed to Healing Arts, after securing Charlotte's solemn oath that Healing Arts meant the same thing to her as Standard Medicine. Jerome returned to the hardware shop for the extra letters.

Last week, I was summoned to a patient of mine from my days at Saint Anne's who had taken a turn for the worse. When I arrived, he proceeded to wretch a black, viscous fluid streaked with blood. Before I could react, he had expelled a torrent across my shirt and trousers. This sort of thing seems to happen to me quite often. I recoiled, but steeled myself to continue the examination. Alas, my efforts were in vain, and the patient succumbed to the fever shortly thereafter.

There are some who say God's healing grace should be reserved for those wealthy enough to receive it, as though wealth were proof of moral worth. I don't share this opinion. Just this morning, Jerome and I were called to the home—hovel, really, which she shared with a dozen other young, destitute people—of an unmarried pregnant woman, her body ravaged by yellow fever. She was mere days from her due date, and we knew that without immediate intervention, both mother and child would succumb. We performed an emergency Cesarean section, a desperate gamble, but her only chance. Tragically, we couldn't save the child, and as I gazed upon the stillborn infant, I had never felt so helpless or so worthless.

I hear you're in poor health. My professional recommendation is that you seek proper medical attention without delay. I know the rift between us has been long and painful, but I wouldn't wish you to suffer needlessly. Please, set aside your pride and allow a qualified physician to tend to your ailments.

Sincerely,

Your Son,

Hiram T. Whitaker

P.S. As I was leaving at the end of the day to take this letter to the post office, I encountered Charlotte, who asked if I'd like some company, seeing that we were headed in the same direction.

As we strolled together, a hearse wagon rumbled past, followed by a distraught woman stumbling after it. Filled with dread—for something about her felt vaguely familiar, even if I couldn't make out who she was at that distance—I decided to follow the procession, and Charlotte came with me. We'd heard the cemeteries were full and were curious to see what would happen when they arrived.

As we neared the gates, a loud crack echoed through the air and we watched in horror as the coffin burst open and its occupant was expelled onto the street by the body's pent-up gases—a grotesque eruption of death's final indignity if ever there was one.

There, lying on the street before us, was the tiny, lifeless form of Antoinette, the girl I had treated at Saint Anne's only weeks earlier, the one who bore so striking a resemblance to my sister Heather. The sight shook me to my core, and I felt as if I'd lost Heather a second time.

Charlotte and I ran to the scene to help the wagon driver lift the child back into the box. After much commotion—and wailing from the girl's mother, Evangeline—the procession continued to St. Louis Cemetery No. 1, only to be turned away and told to go to No. 2. We followed them there and went inside after them.

What I saw beyond those gates will be a part of me forever. Bodies piled high like cords of wood, air thick with the stench of death. Dozens, if not hundreds, of men toiling, digging shallow graves, their shirts soaked through with sweat. They sang as they worked, their voices rising into the evening sky like ghosts. The sound was melancholy and beautiful.

In the end, they found a space for Antoinette, wedging her small body between two adults, her face pressed against an old man's bony back. They sprinkled a handful of lime over them and shoveled barely six inches of dirt over their bodies.

Hiram

Charlotte's hand lingered briefly on my arm before she went on her way to the herb shop.

I walked home, napped fitfully, finished writing the letter, then trudged to the post office. There, I picked up a letter from Patience Dufilho, and, to my surprise and delight, one from Emma Smith. Instead of mailing the letter to my father, I crumpled it into a wad and dropped it into the wastebasket by the door.

Resisting the temptation to open the letters immediately, I strolled home, gripping them tightly, feeling the paper grow damp in my hand. Upstairs, I lit a cigar and poured a glass of whiskey—a combination I'd found worked even better than a cigar alone to help ease my desperate longing for morphine. After my pulse slowed, I opened Patience Dufilho's letter.

Aug 15, 1853

Dearest Hiram,

I write with hope that this letter finds you well and that conditions in our beloved New Orleans have improved. The newspapers paint the bleakest of pictures.

My lawyers and I have been negotiating with Sarah Dufilho and her hideous children, who unfortunately have somehow learned of my beloved Louis's passing. The negotiations have been neither particularly pleasant nor have they gone especially well. Fortunately, these matters take time. Our arrangement regarding the pharmacy remains in place, pending your continued interest.

Regarding Charlotte France's amended will, Sarah's lawyers contest its validity. Miss France likely has more information on the current state of negotiations.

Meeting you was a beacon of hope in those dark days following my husband's passing. For that, I am eternally grateful.

Yours sincerely,

Patience Dufilho

I put down the letter and looked up at the darkening sky. The first stars emerged. Somewhere a dog barked.

Why, I wondered, had I been so fortunate as to meet such a woman just when I needed her most? Perhaps, I was forced to concede, there was some greater power at work, though I had no idea what it might be.

Downing the last of the whiskey, I tore open Emma's letter.

August 12th, 1853 – New York City

Dear Hiram,

That you have received this letter brings me great joy, for it means you have survived. Not a day has passed without me thinking of you. I've carried a terrible guilt for running away without leaving a note, and I hope you didn't waste a moment's time wondering about me.

When I came to work that day in June to find not a living soul in our little hospital, my wits deserted me. I couldn't bear another moment of so much sickness and death. How could it be said that we were accomplishing anything when all our patients—and nearly all of us—were dead? You should have seen me running from room to room, screaming, crying, and then, realizing you weren't there among the dead, laughing hysterically as any madwoman. Which, I suppose, I was.

I couldn't bear it any longer. I ran straight to a riverboat leaving New Orleans. So began an arduous six-week journey where I fell deathly ill with fever, but by God's grace I survived. I am now recovered and working as a nurse at New York Hospital.

This city is free of the pestilence that ravaged New Orleans. I implore you, dear Hiram, from the bottom of my heart, for your own health and happiness, leave that cursed city and come join me in New York, where hope and life still flourish.

God bless you,

Emma

19

I sat at the bar ensconced in the blue haze of cigar smoke, nursing a whiskey, watching mesmerized as Charlotte glided from one partner to another, her every move a magnet for the room's collective gaze. She drew the light to her, catching the warm glow of each flickering candle and casting it back to the room. When I lost sight of her, it was as if clouds had blotted out the sun. And when she reappeared, I felt warm again.

I've probably had too much to drink, I thought, tilting the glass to watch the amber liquid slosh about.

The Quadroon Ball was no longer what it had been when Charlotte's mother, Stella France, met her father, Louis Dufilho, here in 1830. I imagined those nights, full of elegance and opulence, with gentlemen in beaver fur top hats and women in silks that whispered across the floor. Tonight, a few of the men appeared well-to-do, but most were ordinary men, some less than that—with not a beaver fur top hat in sight.

As for the women, if this place had once been the haunt of the most elegant in New Orleans, that could no longer be said—with the obvious exception of Charlotte.

I peered down at my empty glass. How many drinks had I downed? Four? Five at the most. Yet Charlotte had consumed at least ten glasses of champagne by my count, each proffered by a different man desperate to advance through the queue for a dance with her.

What was her secret, I wondered. I would have stumbled to my hands and knees by the sixth or seventh glass.

I left the bar and made my way through the crowd to lean against the wall nearer to Charlotte and her latest partner—a short, homely man whose gaze remained fixed upon her décolletage. As they twirled past, I caught her eyes now and then, and imagined they twinkled more brightly at the sight of me, and that the smile that graced her lips was meant for me alone.

She stumbled.

I pushed off the wall.

She crashed to the floor, her pink taffeta dress swirling around her like cherry blossoms shaken loose by a sudden gust.

I pushed through the crush of bodies, the band's blaring cacophony battering my ears. By the time I reached her, Charlotte's partner was already kneeling beside her, pressing his hands into the folds of her dress, groping at her curves.

I clamped a hand on his shoulder. "Sir, take your hands off her."

Charlotte glared at me from the floor and shook her head.

"But—" I stammered.

"Go away," she mouthed.

I froze. "Is he—"

"Get away from me!" she snapped, aloud this time.

I released the man and backed away, confused, heat rising in my face.

Returning to the bar, I drowned my humiliation in another glass of whiskey. I was desperate to leave, but I had escorted Charlotte here, and I would see her home.

Not long after my retreat, Charlotte emerged from the throng, took the stool beside me, ordered another champagne, and sighed.

"That one always carries a knife," she said, nodding toward the man who had groped her, at the far end of the bar. "He's killed *beaucoup d'hommes* just like you."

From the folds of her dress she produced a small, pearl-colored sachet, tipped its contents into her champagne, and gave the glass a swirl. The pink liquid popped and sparkled.

"Let's not let one *crétin* ruin our night," she said.

"Is that how you keep from getting drunk? Something in that powder?"

She drained half the glass and smiled. "Yes, Doctor Whitaker. You should try it."

She pressed another sachet into my hand, then vanished into the crowd, leaving me alone with the glass and the powder, the air crackling in her wake.

I turned to the mirror behind the bar to study the man who stared back. Why had you come tonight? Was it curiosity about the ball, or something else? To protect her? And if so, why? *What business is it of yours?*

I opened the sachet and upended its contents into the glass. I swirled it, as she had done. The powder dissolved without a trace.

"To your health, old boy," I muttered, then tossed back the ensorcelled whiskey. A strange effervescence tingled against my tongue.

Moments later, as if sensing I'd taken her tonic, Charlotte seized my hand and pulled me onto the dance floor. As we waltzed, so too did my emotions. My head swam and I felt as though I were floating on air. Being so close to her, her body pressed against mine, her warmth seeping through the layers of fabric, filled me with a dizzying joy I hadn't felt in a long time.

Soon, the faces surrounding us blurred and disappeared. The flickering candle flames became stars in the heavens. The music faded, replaced by the rhythm of our breath and the beating of our hearts. There was only Charlotte and me, two stars orbiting each other as they spun through the cosmos.

A planet appeared in the distance. As we neared, its surface details sharpened—mountain forests, rolling hills, a desert stretching out like a sea of bone-white sand.

There, on the edge between green and white, stood Mary Beth, small and fragile against the vastness. At her feet lay my body, or the body of someone who looked like me, still and lifeless.

She sat beside it and took my hand, holding it as Charlotte and I—there must have been two of me, the dying one and the living—spun round and round.

Mary Beth, still holding my hand, lay down beside me and closed her eyes. I opened mine, sat up, and let go of her hand, as I let go of Charlotte's.

I stood to look down at Mary Beth as Charlotte drifted away into the arms of another man. And I, finding myself no longer in the desert nor the heavens, made my way back to the bar, where every stool was taken. I stood there awhile, looking down at my brown leather shoes and the memory of Mary Beth, which no amount of spiked whiskey or dancing could erase.

"Let go of me, Albert." Charlotte's words cut through the noise. "Let go!" she cried again.

I saw her through the haze of smoke and swirling bodies. A man in a tuxedo held her pinned against the wall. She struggled, but he gripped her by the shoulders and slammed her back.

"Dance with me, you octoroon bitch!"

Before I even knew I'd left the bar, my fist connected with the man's ear. There was a burst of red, and he crumpled to the floor. Someone grabbed my shoulder and spun me around. I tried to dodge the blow, but his fist crashed into my cheek and glanced across my lips. Stars burst behind my eyes and the hot, metallic taste of blood filled my mouth.

Somehow, Charlotte's hand found mine, and we ran.

Angry shouts echoed behind us as we raced down the stairs and into the night. We laughed wildly, our feet pounding the earth until we collapsed onto a bench in Père Antoine's garden, gasping for breath. The cathedral loomed behind us, its spires piercing the smoke-filled sky. The night closed in, and the world fell silent. For a fleeting moment, nothing else existed.

"That was most fun, wasn't it, Doctor Whitaker?" Charlotte said, breathless.

"It was indeed," I replied, the tang of blood still lingering on my tongue.

She reached into her décolletage and pulled out a bill-fold, which she opened to reveal twenty-two dollars, a small fortune.

"A little gift from that man on the floor," she said. She pocketed the cash and tossed the empty billfold into the bushes. "I hope you don't mind."

I had no objections, only admiration. Maybe even awe. "Not at all."

She smiled. Then, with a flourish, she produced another billfold, and then another.

"This one's a gift from Albert," she said, holding up the fourth.

All told, she'd netted us nearly sixty dollars.

"Have you been to that fancy new restaurant, Antoine's?" she asked.

"I've never been to any fancy restaurant."

"Then let's go." She slipped the money into a hidden pocket in her dress. "I'm famished. My treat."

As we strolled along Royal Street, the gas lamps casting long, flickering shadows that swayed across the rain-slicked cobblestones, a figure stepped out from the darkness and tipped his hat.

"Evening, Miss Charlotte. Doctor."

"Evening, Baron," Charlotte replied.

I managed a brief nod. Our eyes met for an instant before he receded once more into the shadows, his tall, lanky frame swallowed by the night as though he'd never been there at all.

I awoke to shafts of sunlight peeking through the curtains. Rubbing the sleep from my eyes, I became aware of the sweet, woodsy aroma of bayberry. I sat up and noticed a candle flickering on the nightstand. Inhaling deeply, I felt a sense of renewal, even optimism. Swinging my legs over the side of the bed, I realized with surprise that there was no trace of pain or stiffness from the previous night's brawling. Puzzled, I crossed to the mirror above the mantel, between two vases of dead flowers, to stare at my reflection. No bruises, no lacerations; the cuts on my cheek and lip had completely healed.

Drawn by the aroma of coffee, I descended the stairs and stepped into the courtyard, where Jerome sat on the bench by the fountain, engrossed in a book. He looked up as I approached.

"There you are," he said, slipping a ribbon between the pages. "I was beginning to think you'd sleep the day away."

I shaded my eyes and glanced at the sun angling toward the west. It must have been three, maybe four in the afternoon. I sat down on the opposite bench, in the dappled shade of the magnolia.

"Coffee?" Jerome offered, already rising.

"Please."

He soon returned with a cup. I took a sip. It tasted—not of happiness, precisely, but of something like it. Contentment, maybe, along with something else I couldn't place. Regardless, I felt instantly revived. I considered asking him what he'd put in it, but decided against it.

"What are you reading?" I asked instead.

"*Uncle Tom's Cabin.* My third time through."

"I've heard of it. Is it really that good?"

"Maybe if you read something besides that *United States Pharmacopeia*, you'd know how good it is."

"Maybe someday," I said. "What's it about?"

"Slavery."

I nodded. "Anything more specific?"

"About a black man called Uncle Tom who endures vicious beatings by one of his masters but never loses his faith in God."

"The twin shackles of slavery and religion. Not that I wish to equate the two. But there are certainly—"

"*Oui*," Jerome interrupted. "They are not the same thing."

I nodded and let it go.

"It's also about a girl called Eliza, who escapes to freedom before her owner can sell her son Harry to pay off his debts."

"How does she pull it off?"

"She takes him in her arms and runs across the frozen Ohio River, leaping from ice floe to ice floe as they rush down the river, until some people help them up the bank on the other side."

"It makes it sound so easy."

"In the book, it's presented as a miracle."

"Hmm. Yes."

We sat without speaking for a while, sipping our coffee, the fountain trickling softly.

Jerome tilted his head toward the sky. "Looks like the weather's clearing up."

"I'm sorry your sister Arabella wasn't so fortunate, Jerome... as that girl Eliza in the book."

His eyes remained fixed on a passing cloud. "Me too," he said.

"I wish there was something I could do." The inadequacy of my words bothered me. What good was wishing something if I didn't intend to do something about it? "What becomes of Uncle Tom himself?"

He looked away from the clouds and studied me. "You want me to tell you how the story ends?"

I shrugged, then nodded.

"He gives up everything to stay true to his beliefs. To do what he believes is right."

"Everything?"

He nodded, then opened the book to the marked page.

I watched him for a moment, then took another sip of coffee. "This coffee is very good," I said, before he could lose himself in the book again. I'd changed my mind, I would ask. "What's in it? I can't place the flavor."

"Devil's shoestring," he said, without looking up.

"Devil's—?"

"Good for the digestion."

"Ah."

I leaned back and let my eyes wander to the magnolia tree's canopy. Sunlight caught the edges of its leaves, etching them in silver.

"I heard you're quite the dancer, Doc."

"You did?"

"Charlotte said dancing with you was like whirling through the stars."

I coughed, nearly choking on my coffee.

"Yes," I said. "We had a nice time together."

"Sounds like it."

He tried again to return to his book.

"Jerome?"

He glanced up. "Yes?"

"What is it, exactly?"

"What's what?"

"Voodoo."

"Oh."

"I know it's some sort of Haitian-African magic, with a bit of the Catholic thrown in for good measure. But I don't really get the gist of it."

"It's not magic, Doc. It's religion, with its own beliefs and practices. Just like any religion."

"But belief in what, exactly? And what practices? There must be more to it than powdered bones, Tarot cards, and gris-gris bags."

He sighed. "We—they—believe in nature, that's all. The earth, the water, the sky."

I felt a flicker of annoyance; there had to be more to it than believing in the earth and the sky. Still, I was in a good enough mood and I wanted to keep things civil.

"Unlike angels, saints, and ghosts, those things can be seen and touched," I said. "They're real."

"Oh? You can touch the sky?"

"I can see the sky."

"People see ghosts and saints, too."

"No, they do not."

"They believe they do. Just as you believe you see the sky."

I shook my head. "Jerome, you and I both know—"

"It's not just belief, Doctor Whitaker. It's a reverence for the gifts of the universe. Every tree, root, plant, and animal has its own spirit, with its own power to affect our lives."

While I doubted the spirit of any tree had ever affected my life, I appreciated Jerome's willingness to try to explain it to me. "Go on," I said. "What else?"

"They believe the ancestors walk among us and guide us and protect us. If we honor them."

"Hmm."

"I take it you don't believe in such things."

"That's true."

"And yet you may find yourself guided by your memories of lost relatives and loved ones, even if you haven't thought about it that way."

At these words, I felt a pang.

"And so you try to honor them," he went on. "To avoid doing things they'd disapprove of, and to do things that would make them proud. As if they were watching you, guiding you."

I had the faint impression that, rather than being informed, I was being hypnotized, both by his words and the movements of his hands as he spoke.

"I suppose that's true," I said.

"Couldn't it be said, then, that their spirits guide your decisions and affect your actions?"

"Memories aren't the same things as spirits. But I take your point."

"Maybe they are, maybe they aren't. Pending further scientific testing, of course," he said with a smile.

"What about loas? A fortune teller once told me I had strong ones looking after me, but I've no idea what that means. Not that I believe the words of a fortune teller."

"Of course you don't. You're an educated white man from the North."

"Well then, what are they?"

"They're like saints and angels—divine forces who govern our health, love, fertility, life and death. We pay them homage. We build relationships with them."

"Through prayer?"

"Prayer. Chanting, magic, dancing."

"You said it wasn't magic."

He shrugged.

"Gris-gris bags, voodoo dolls, and such?" I said dryly.

He reached into his pocket and pulled out an amulet. "Protection and healing." He pointed to the sky. "Papa Loko, O!"

I shook my head. How could such an intelligent man believe in such nonsense?

He slipped the amulet back into his pocket.

"We've used these things for thousands of years, Doc. Because they work. Isn't that what science is?"

"Yes. But—"

"Can something be false if it works? Can something be true if it doesn't?"

"No."

"Yet most of your medical science isn't supported by any evidence at all. Just the opposite. You accept it despite proof it *doesn't* work. You take it on faith."

"That isn't true at all."

"You've been at this for a year or two. I've been at it for more than twenty. And I'll tell you God's honest truth—what you believe rests on that alone: your belief. When your eyes are confronted with the truth, you shut them. You shut your mind, too, and carry on, desperate to confirm the rightness of your faith in the *United States Phar-macopeia*, no matter the cost."

He paused, then added, more quietly: "Whatever animates this willful blindness, only you can say."

Jerome's words tested my patience, yet I resolved to keep my composure. People spellbound by ridiculous notions could no more be argued with than could a butterfly or a blade of grass.

I took a sip of coffee and let it settle me, then looked up to watch the clouds drift by. How peaceful and light they were, untouched by worry, unburdened by earthly foolishness.

Once I'd calmed, I asked, "What about the Catholic angle? I've noticed a lot of you go to church."

He nodded. "That's true."

"Your loas and such aren't enough?"

He shrugged.

"You know what I don't understand?" I said. "How does a man savagely subjugated in the name of another man's God come to embrace that God so fervently? I'd think he'd reject it outright."

"You're right, we adopted many things from the French colonists who enslaved us. But we weren't allowed to practice our own traditions, so we hid them in theirs. We had our own rosary beads, sacraments, chants, and regalia. But we had to let theirs stand in for ours. Same with the saints and the loas. The Virgin Mary was our Erzulie Freda, loa of love and feminine beauty. Saint Peter, who holds the keys to the Kingdom of Heaven, became our Papa Legba, gatekeeper between worlds. Their Holy Trinity became our three faces of Bondye, the unknowable God. It's no big leap; after all, saints intercede the same way as loas do. But to answer your question: many of these things blended and became one and the same. More coffee, Docteur?"

"Yes, why not? I suppose a little devil's shoestring never hurt anyone."

20

Dear Hiram,

I write this letter on behalf of your father, William. But also as his nurse on behalf of myself.

You are a man of medicine so I will begin by sharing the dry facts of your father's condition. He suffers from fever, chills, night sweats, chest pains, and labored breathing. He has weakened to the point of being bedridden all day. His body is wracked by a persistent, ragged cough that brings up phlegm streaked with blood. His physician, Dr. Cartwright, has diagnosed consumption and prescribed cod liver oil, creosote, beef tea, laudanum, and leeching. Other than the tea, your father refuses these treatments.

But as in all things, there are more than just the dry facts to consider. I believe, as a nurse, we must treat the patient's whole being, for he is more than his body alone. He is the sum of his experiences, memories, emotions, hopes, dreams, and regrets. This is certainly true of your father, who has taken me not only into his physical but also spiritual confidence. I assure you, whichever disease may rot his body, it has not rotted his heart, regardless of what you may believe.

I will update you on any changes in his condition. Until then, may the Lord's embrace bring you peace.

Yours in service,

Bridget O'Malley – your father's nurse

I folded the letter, held it to the lamp's flame, and watched it burn.

To hell with my father's *whole being*.

Later that day, after checking on a few patients, I returned home to find Jerome tinkering with the soda machine. Flavored sodas masked the bitterness of quinine, iron tonic, and bark laxatives. We still offered the standard flavors—blueberry, strawberry, vanilla, and sarsaparilla—that Louis Dufilho had always provided. But Charlotte had recently suggested we branch out to set ours apart from the other apothecaries in town.

"What do you propose?" I'd asked, skeptical but willing to hear her out.

"Lemon, lime, any refreshing citrus. Maybe some other things, too."

"What sort of other things?"

"This and that," she'd said, with maddening vagueness.

"Lemon and lime are as bitter as quinine," I'd pointed out. "How is that supposed to help?"

"That's why you add lots of cane sugar."

Now, Jerome tinkered at the soda machine with various ingredients, none of which appeared to be blueberry, strawberry, sarsaparilla, or vanilla.

"Try this," he said, handing me a glass of bubbling soda with a yellowish hue.

I took a sip. It fizzed pleasantly on my tongue—brightly citrusy at first, but with an unexpected depth. I drank again, trying to discern the flavors.

"Charlotte's lemon-lime," I said.

"You got it, Doc. What do you think?"

"Not as good as vanilla or blueberry, of course. Palatable."

He rinsed the glass, scooped in a dollop of dark syrup, added soda and a tablespoon of sugar, then stirred. "Try this one."

Eager to get this over with—blueberry and strawberry were perfectly adequate—I took a big mouthful. The taste was peculiar but undeniably good. Citrusy again, but with something exotic layered in which I couldn't identify. I thought Jerome might be onto something.

"What is it?" I asked. "I've never tasted anything quite like it."

He grinned. "Good, isn't it?"

"Not terrible. What's in it?"

"Florida water."

"Never heard of it."

"It was Charlotte's idea. Apparently it's quite common in some circles."

"It's not some sort of—"

"Wards off evil spirits," Jerome said.

"Wonderful."

"Mediums use it to communicate with the ancestors and anoint their third eye."

"No wonder it's so delicious: it tastes perfectly of anointed third eye."

Jerome stared at me, evidently surprised at my attempt at humor.

"What's in it, this Florida water?" I asked. "Lizard bones? Snake hearts? Cemetery dirt?"

He checked the recipe on a piece of paper. "Orange and lemon oil, nutmeg, cinnamon, coriander, neroli oil—that's bitter orange blossom—vanilla. The main ingredient is kola nut. Gives it that unusual flavor."

"Never heard of that, either."

"Charlotte says her mother used it in her Healing, Protection, and Love potion. Big seller. But the important thing is, it tastes good."

I shook my head slowly.

"It's not a voodoo potion, Doc. It's just a soda to make your toxic laxatives go down with less suffering."

"Whatever it is, it's delicious."

He smiled. "You had me worried for a minute."

"We should offer it to our customers right away," I said.

"You really think so?"

"And we mustn't let on that it's Florida water and sugar," I said. "Let's see how they like it."

"I'll mix up a batch tonight and we can start offering it tomorrow."

"You know," I said, feeling inspired by the remarkable flavor, "I have an idea. What if we sprinkled in a touch of cocaine to give it a little extra kick, and marketed it as a remedy in its own right?"

Jerome laughed. "Are you serious? I'm not sure I saw 'cocaine and kola' in your *Pharmacopeia*."

"I've visited a few other apothecaries around town to see what they're offering. Everyone has their own concoction. Why shouldn't we? We'll call it Doctor Whitaker's Cures-all."

"I have a better idea. Let's call it Coca-Kola."

I laughed. It felt good to share a lighthearted moment with Jerome. "Let's not get ahead of ourselves. If we call it Coca-Kola, everyone in town will know what's in it and steal our formula."

"That's true. All right, Doctor Whitaker's Cures-all it is. I'll start mixing up a batch right now."

The man's name was J.T. Farmer, Esquire, counselor at law, according to his business card. He was of medium height, stocky build, and dressed in fine wool garments. A black bowler hat shaded his green eyes, which shone above a thick blond mustache.

We sat in his office, a cramped upstairs room on Saint Charles Avenue. Leather-bound legal volumes lined the walls, interrupted only by oil portraits of important-looking men.

"Decided I'd try my luck and come back to town," Farmer said. "Might regret it, but I was getting bored up at my mother's house. As for Sarah Dufilho and those New York people, they're full of bluster. My client's position is as solid as the Rock of Gibraltar. Put your faith in it."

His client being Charlotte France.

"As to why Sarah and Patience Dufilho didn't know about Mr. Dufilho's amended will, it's simple: he didn't want them to know.

"Sir William Blackstone," he said, catching me staring at the painting behind him, a red-cloaked man with a corpulent face and long, curly white wig. "Finest legal mind ever to illuminate the dark bowels of jurisprudence."

"Ah."

"The only complication for Miss France is that the will stipulates she'll receive twenty-five percent of the proceeds upon Louis Dufilho's death; but it doesn't specify whether the sale must be immediate. Lawsuits are a distinct possibility."

"But if all parties agreed to sell immediately, then Miss France would receive twenty-five percent?"

"Yes, sir."

"And if she preferred to keep the property, whether as an investment or a residence?"

"From what I know of Sarah Dufilho, she won't agree to that."

It wasn't the news I'd hoped for. I left Farmer's office with a knot in my stomach, agitated and increasingly uneasy about our tenure at the Chartres Street townhouse.

* * *

I learned from Jerome that most slaves were granted a semblance of freedom on Sundays, within limits that had been tightened in recent years. This respite typically included attending church and the dances in Congo Square. But he rarely saw his sister, Arabella, who was usually confined to the McFarland residence, even on Sundays.

In the days and weeks after her attempted escape, Jerome held little hope of seeing her at all. Still, he managed to glean fragments of news from people who worked with her or knew someone who did.

On this damp, warm Sunday evening in early September, Jerome met with the sister of one of McFarland's cooks. He returned home before darkness fell; slaves, and even free people of color, were subject to harassment and arrest if caught outside after a certain hour.

He joined me for a smoke on my balcony just as the sun began to set.

"Did you find out anything?" I asked, holding a flame to his cigar.

He puffed until the ember glowed, then looked at me with a grim expression, as if weighing whether I was too delicate to hear the truth.

"Thirty lashes to her back, ten to her legs," he said. "Punched her in the face and chest. Broke her nose and a few ribs. Spared the baby."

Even after a year in New Orleans, stories like this still filled me with rage.

"I can't accept it," I said. "People owning other people, treating them worse than dogs. Yes, it's in the Bible, I know that. But this isn't Egypt. We live in the modern world, not the Biblical one. There must be a solution."

"Solution to what, exactly?"

"Your sister's..." I glanced around, as if unseen ears might be listening from the shadows. "Unfortunate situation."

Jerome rested his cigar in the ashtray. "And what might that solution entail?"

"What if I bought Arabella from McFarland?"

He shook his head. "She's not for sale."

"Everything has a price."

"He's owned her since she was three. Others have tried to buy her. He's not selling. At any price."

I sighed.

The sun had gone down, leaving the streets below bathed in a dark, reddish glow. A cool breeze stirred the air.

"Isn't there some way to help her escape to a free state? Like that girl in the book?"

Jerome stood and gripped the balcony railing. He scanned the street, then turned to me. "We can both get strung up for this kind of talk, Doc. Or beaten to death in Jackson Square. Set on fire while white people laugh and cheer and throw their shit at our burning bodies."

I nodded and looked up at the orange clouds in the purpling sky. What kind of hell had I stumbled into in this godforsaken town, I wondered, not for the first time, nor even the tenth.

21

The leaves turned vibrant shades of gold, orange, and red, and with them so too did our fortunes take on a different hue. The fever abated. The desperation that once drove patients to our medical practice began to wane. Other hospitals reopened with beds to spare, drawing away some of our more critical cases. Not that we lacked for patients—there was still no shortage of the poor relying on our affordable services—but the daily crush ebbed to a more manageable flow.

Yet our apothecary, managed by Charlotte, grew more prosperous by the day. She took the occasional day off beyond her usual Sunday—when she wasn't feeling well, or had private matters to attend to—and on those days, fewer people stepped through our doors. When they did, they always asked after Miss Charlotte, their faces falling when I told them she was out for the day. I would hasten to add that I was perfectly capable of filling their prescriptions or recommending medicines, but my assurances rarely seemed to lift their spirits.

It wasn't only the men who inquired about Miss Charlotte with ill-disguised disappointment upon being informed of her absence. Even the society matrons and Creole ladies seeking tinctures and ointments lost some of their sparkle when I, rather than Charlotte, stepped up to assist them at the counter.

One slow afternoon, I lingered in the apothecary re-arranging displays, flipping through the ledgers, adjusting the colored apothecary globes in the window—all the while keeping an eye on Charlotte's interactions with our cus-tomers. Now and then, I watched her compound pills, not-ing which containers she drew the ingredients from. As far as I could tell, there was nothing unusual about her prepa-rations.

Eventually, tiring of my observations, I made my way to-ward the rear door, intending to go upstairs to study the *Pharmacopeia*. But just as my hand reached the door han-dle, the bell above the entrance jingled, and a woman I rec-ognized as one of my patients stepped inside. Her face lit up at the sight of Charlotte behind the counter. But when her gaze drifted to the shadows at the back of the room where I stood, her smile faltered.

"Good afternoon, Mrs. Meriwether," I called out.

"Good afternoon, Doctor Whitaker," she replied cheer-ily.

"What can we help you with today?"

She and Charlotte exchanged a fleeting glance, one I might have missed had I not been watching closely.

"I've come for more of those arsenic and mercury pills you prescribed, doctor. They've worked wonders for my lady troubles."

"Glad to hear it, Mrs. Meriwether."

Satisfied that all was in order, I turned and left through the rear door, leaving Charlotte to fill the prescription.

That Saturday evening, Charlotte joined Jerome and me for dinner in the kitchen. Jerome was making his famous red beans and rice, a dish Charlotte swore she wouldn't miss even if her life depended on it.

Since the day I'd observed her compounding medicines, she'd seemed distant, and I wanted to mend our relationship. As I watched her laugh at one of Jerome's stories, I considered asking if she might like to take a stroll with me through the Quarter. Perhaps we could do a little window shopping along Royal Street, or simply enjoy the evening air together.

"What are your plans for after church tomorrow?" I asked, striving to sound casual as Jerome served his renowned beans and rice.

"Paying my respects at the cemetery," Charlotte replied.

"Oh? Did someone die?"

"Yes. Someone died. My mother."

My cheeks burned. "Of course. I'm sorry."

She shook her head.

It struck me then that I had never asked her about her mother, or how the loss had affected her, even as I dwelled on the absence of my own. I apologized again, then hesitated before asking, "Would you mind if I joined you?"

To my surprise, she said, "I would like that very much."

The next day, I waited outside Saint Louis Cathedral. After services ended, Charlotte emerged amidst a gaggle of her elegantly dressed friends. Watching them chatter animatedly, I found it difficult—painful, even—to reconcile that many of these vibrant people were the legal property of men like J.W. McFarland. That there was nothing I could do about it gnawed at me incessantly.

Eventually, Charlotte's friends drifted off toward Congo Square, and she joined me in the shade of a sprawling oak. From there, we began our stroll.

"I wanted to tell you how sorry I am about—" I began.

"You don't trust me," she said.

I stopped, but she walked on, and I hurried to catch up.

"What do you mean? Of course I trust you."

"You think I'm mixing voodoo potions instead of something from that big black book of yours."

"Not at all," I lied.

We paused at the corner of St. Louis and Bourbon streets as a wagon loaded with crates of bananas rumbled past. How strange to see a cart piled high with bright yellow fruit instead of caskets. Could life really be returning to normal? It seemed so, yet it was difficult to believe.

"Business is good, isn't it?" Charlotte said, as we stepped around the filth in the street.

"Very good," I agreed. "We've been quite profitable lately."

"People seem to favor what I sell them."

"Yes, it would seem so," I said, wary of where this was going.

We stopped at a florist's kiosk to purchase bouquets of purple irises and white oleander for her mother's grave.

"If I sold them sassafras and mandrake instead of mercury, because mercury makes them feel bad, and sassafras and mandrake make them feel good, what would you say to that?"

"I'd say there's no evidence for the efficacy of—"

"Do you even listen to yourself speak sometimes?"

"Of course I do."

We resumed our walk, bouquets in hand.

"Voodoo holds no scientific merit," I said. "I'm trying to run a legitimate apothecary. If any of your potions and powders make someone feel better, it's only because they believe it will. It's not real medicine. It doesn't cure anything. It—"

Charlotte stopped. I knew I'd gone too far, and I wished I could take it back.

"You are, *sans aucun doute*, the most ridiculous man I have ever known, Monsieur Whitaker. And that is saying something—for I have known many, many ridiculous men."

"I'm sorry if I—"

"You leech people's blood and burn their flesh with mustard to relieve their foot pain. You make them shit their guts out to cure their chicken pox. You induce them to vomit until they're green in the face because it hurts when they pee. Can't you see how barbaric it all is?"

"Those are the accepted, proven medical—"

She shook her head. "Don't."

We walked the rest of the way in silence, past old women selling ice cream and cupcakes, and children playing with whirligigs—wooden spools on strings they spun down and whipped back with a flick of the wrist. The lively street scene faded behind us as we stepped through the cemetery gates into a world of death.

What is death? I wondered, as we passed by groups of men trying to fit one more body into the ground, where there was no room left, not even for babies, now pressed together like sardines in a tin. Did death end when mourning did? Were my mother and sister still dead only because I continued to mourn them? Could they move on to some other realm if I stopped? Could I ever?

And what would become of my rage when Father was gone, when there was no one left to receive it? What would become of my despair when its architect ceased to be?

We wove our way through clusters of the grieving until we reached a mound in the cemetery's northwest corner, marked by a plain wooden cross. Wildflowers, abuzz with bees, grew around it. A gentle breeze carried the stench of death, mingling with the faint sweetness of the flowers.

This, I thought, was the true smell of New Orleans: sweetness and death.

We laid the bouquets on the mound. I stepped back as Charlotte knelt and spoke to her mother in French. When she finished, she drew a jar from her purse, scooped a handful of dirt from the grave into it, sealed it, and tucked it away.

"What's that for?" I asked.

"Voodoo spells."

We held each other's gaze a moment before her features softened into a smile. "Don't you possess even a lick of humor, Doctor Whitaker?"

"I suppose I must, once in a while. But something about these surroundings leaves me feeling humorless."

"It's for the flowers on my balcony," she said. "It helps them grow."

On the way home, we stopped at a small grocery store with a butcher shop in the back. Such places had been short of merchandise or shuttered entirely during the early months of the epidemic, but this one had well-stocked shelves—another sign that life was inching back to normal.

As I browsed rows of canned goods, Charlotte approached the counter and spoke quietly with the butcher, an older black man in a bloodstained apron. I paid little attention at first, captivated as I was by the variety of canned tomatoes arrayed before me. Stewed, crushed, diced, puréed, whole peeled. Which of these, I wondered, might inspire Jerome to prepare one of his delectable Creole dishes? Perhaps Charlotte would know.

I turned down the aisle to ask her when I caught fragments of their conversation.

"Un homme égaré," she said softly. A misguided man.

To whom was she referring?

"Un homme perdu. Mais un homme bon." A lost man. But a good man.

"Quelque chose en lui, dont il refuse de parler, le blesse profondément." Something inside of him, which he refuses to talk about, hurts him deeply.

"J'ai hâte qu'il se sente mieux. Mais il s'est endurci." I long for him to feel better. But he has hardened himself.

"Oui, le cœur de bœuf est très frais aujourd'hui," the butcher said, noticing me. Yes, the beef heart is very fresh today.

I felt guilty for eavesdropping on them, even if I had never explicitly told Charlotte I didn't understand French.

I purchased a large can of whole peeled tomatoes, and Charlotte bought a beef heart. As we walked home, I asked what one does with such a thing. The idea of eating it struck me as ghastly.

"One makes voodoo spells," she replied.

I hesitated, caught between a laugh and the fear of proving her right. Hard and humorless. Who could resist such a man? At least Emma had found me decent enough to write a letter to, even if she had left without a word. And Charlotte, despite everything, had called me a good man. That much was something to be grateful for.

Lost in these thoughts, I almost missed the tall figure standing in the shadows of an alley. Recognizing him, I stopped and tipped my hat, and he returned the gesture. Noticing I was no longer beside her, Charlotte stopped. I nodded toward the alley, and she rejoined me.

"Lovely day, ain't it?" Baron Sunday said. "Lovely as the day is long."

"Lovely indeed," I replied.

"Well, hello there, Baron," Charlotte said.

"Hello there, Miss Charlotte. You're looking even more delectable than usual today. Must be that beef heart you're carrying in that bag. Brings out something in a woman, a beef heart does."

"I'm surprised I didn't notice you when we passed," she said.

"Your gentleman friend here, *le docteur*, noticed me right away. Seems he's got a keen eye for things hidden in the darkness."

Charlotte glanced at me. I shrugged. Sunday's shadow had caught my eye, that was all.

Just then, a black cat with one white paw appeared at Sunday's feet.

Charlotte crouched and extended her hand. "Who's your little friend?"

"That's Napoleon, my lucky cat. Never leaves my side."

We exchanged a few pleasantries about the weather before taking our leave. Two blocks from home, I glanced over my shoulder. Napoleon was following us, half a block back.

"Look," I said.

We stopped. The little cat ran to catch up, then trotted alongside us the rest of the way. At the apothecary, he tried to slip inside with us.

"No," I said, gently nudging him outside with my foot and closing the door.

He glanced up and down the street, but decided to stay put on the sidewalk, just outside the door.

"What are you doing? Let the poor thing in," Charlotte said.

"He isn't our cat. He's Baron Sunday's. Besides, this is no place for a cat."

Charlotte crossed her arms. "It's a *purrrfect* place for a cat. Let him in."

"They're disease carriers. For all we know, he's carrying smallpox, rabies, even plague."

"May I remind you that I'm part owner of this building?" she said.

"That remains unsettled."

"And that you are the tenant, nothing more? If the cat wants to come in, the cat is coming in."

"For now, I am the leaseholder, and you are the subletter. Nothing more," I replied.

"Do you wish your subletter to leave?"

"I do not."

"Then the cat is coming in. And don't be foolish. They kill rats. Which, in case they didn't teach you anything in medical college, are the real carriers of the plague. Rats, not cats."

I might have been hardened, even lost, but I was certain of one thing: I didn't want a voodoo cat living in my apothecary. True, he was an attractive little thing, with his white whiskers, golden eyes, and that one white paw. It was just that—

I looked at Charlotte. I had never seen her look so resolute: hands planted on hips, jaw set, lips pressed into a hard line.

"Fine," I said.

I pulled the door open. Napoleon scampered inside and followed us out to the courtyard.

22

Within days, Napoleon became nearly as popular with our clientele as Charlotte herself. Yet I couldn't shake the guilt of having deprived Baron Sunday of his closest companion.

One evening, as I escorted my last patient to the door—a Mrs. Ringsworth, who had severed the tip of her index finger while chopping celery during a spat with her husband (who had declined to accompany her)—I noticed Napoleon sitting in the front window display between the yellow and green apothecary globes. He glanced back at me, his golden eyes meeting mine. It was clear he wanted to go outside.

I felt a pang at the thought he might wish to return to Baron Sunday. Apparently, I hadn't realized how attached I'd become to this charming little animal. Yet I knew I had to honor his wishes. I opened the door, and he leapt down from the display and slipped out onto the banquette. I followed him out and locked the door behind us.

The air was thick with the scent of magnolias, rotting garbage, and something else I couldn't place. Napoleon trotted ahead, his black fur stark against the warm hues of the setting sun. I had no particular destination in mind, but hoped he might lead us toward the river, where we could enjoy the sunset together. Instead, he led us in the direction of Baron Sunday's alley.

"Wouldn't you prefer to go down to the river, little cat?" I said, as we paused for a carriage to rumble past. "Maybe you could catch us a fish for dinner."

Napoleon wasn't having it. He led us onward toward the alley. But just when I expected him to turn up Orleans Street, he veered into the gardens behind the cathedral. Perhaps, I thought, he was drawn by the source of that elusive fragrance wafting on the breeze.

As we ventured deeper into the garden, Napoleon suddenly darted off the path and disappeared into the dense foliage. I followed after him.

That's when I saw her.

She was hidden among the bushes, but Napoleon had gone straight to her. Her eyes were open, glassy and jaundiced. Her skin, the color of cocoa, glistened with dampness. She was young, perhaps twenty. Her green dress clung to her swollen belly—she was heavily pregnant, probably only days from her time.

I stood motionless. She wasn't the first dead pregnant woman I'd encountered, but there was something profoundly tragic about her. Her young life, and that of her unborn child, seemed to hang in the air like an unfinished lullaby.

I knelt to search for a pulse but felt nothing. I pressed an ear to her chest, straining to hear any faint sign of life, but there was only the oppressive silence of death. Her skin was still warm; it seemed she had died only minutes before Napoleon found her. I leaned back and sighed.

As I struggled to overcome the surge of grief welling up inside me, Napoleon climbed onto the dead woman's belly and sat there, standing guard over the baby within. His eyes met mine, unblinking, as if challenging me to act. After a moment, his tail began to twitch rhythmically.

Was he trying to tell me something?

I sat there feeling useless and miserable, as Napoleon's tail twitched on, interspersed with longer waves, as if he were beating out a message in Morse code.

"What are you trying to tell me, little cat?"

His tail twitched, waved.

"I can't help her," I said.

Twitch. Wave.

"It's too late. Even you can see that."

Twitch.

On our walk home, I flagged down a watchman to report our grim discovery. He assured me he'd "look into it," but struck me as thoroughly disinterested, as if yet another dead black woman with an unborn child were of no particular concern to anyone.

23

For a few days after our discovery in the cathedral gardens —and certain events that followed—life settled into its usual rhythm, and I found myself less burdened by the unhappy thoughts that had consumed me for so long. My new quarters were comfortable, even homey, and I took real pleasure in Jerome's cooking and Charlotte's company.

The relative peace of those days, however, was broken by J.W. McFarland's latest unannounced visit, this time accompanied by an associate from the Medical Board, one Thomas Williams, a squat, barrel-chested man whose massive handlebar mustache threatened to devour the lower half of his face.

While Charlotte and I stood by, McFarland and Williams examined instruments, sniffed vials, tasted powders, and leafed through case notes.

"Williams here is aware of our little licensing arrangement," McFarland said at some point.

"Is that so?" I replied, surprised he'd disclosed our agreement to an associate.

"He understands it's provisional," McFarland added, just as Williams shoveled a spoonful of cocaine from a canister into his left nostril and sniffed deeply.

"Seems sufficient quality," Williams said.

"Of course it is," I replied. "We offer only the finest preparations here at Whitaker's."

He wiped the excess powder from his nostrils, then gave Charlotte a lingering look which I didn't appreciate.

"I recognize your girl," he said. "Worked with her mama at a voodoo joint over on Rampart Street. Not peddling that same monkey business here, I trust."

"This is a medical apothecary, Mr. Williams, not a witchcraft shop. I've discussed it with Miss France, and she's assured me of her trustworthiness in this matter."

"I wouldn't be in such a hurry to take the word of a negress if I were you," Williams replied. "They'll say whatever it takes to get what they want. I'd trust my dog before I'd trust a colored girl."

"Miss France is a skilled compounder," I said. "She adheres to the strictest pharmaceutical standards in New Orleans. Whatever superstition she may have been involved in with her mother, she knows perfectly well that if she tried such a thing here, she'd be out on the street."

Williams snorted. "Rather doubt it."

I frowned. "And why is that, Mr. Williams?"

"I heard she owns the place, that's why."

"What say we go up and inspect the medical facilities?" McFarland said, evidently eager to prevent further conflict between Williams and me.

"Bravo," Williams replied, clapping his hands together. "I've had enough of these musty vials."

The three of us went upstairs. While McFarland and Williams poked and prodded at various tools and containers, I stepped out to the balcony to steady my nerves with a cigar.

Half an hour later, as they were leaving, and having found nothing out of order, McFarland stopped in the doorway.

"Something bothering that slave of yours, Whicket?"

"Why do you ask?"

"Didn't like the way he was looking at me. Seems he's got something on his mind."

I hesitated, then spoke plainly. "You know exactly why Jerome looks at you that way."

"Do I?"

"He doesn't care for the way you treat his sister, Arabella."

"Is that so? Yes, I suppose it is. And what of it, Hiram T. Whicket? You know, I've always wondered what the 'T' stood for."

"Sell her to me," I said. The words came out suddenly, though I'd been harboring the notion for some time. "She doesn't deserve what you do to her. No one does."

His eyes widened. "Sell—" He shook his head. "Jesus Christ. I'd sell myself to a fool like you before I'd sell you Arabella."

"Name your price. I'll pay it."

He looked upward, then at me, stepping closer to jab a stiff finger against my chest.

"I believe you've fallen under your nigger's spell, Whicket. Both your niggers' spells. They've got you under their dark thrall like the woolly-brained Northerner you are."

"I'm under no one's thrall. I want to do the right thing —the thing you seem utterly incapable of."

He scoffed and shook his head. "If you want to continue working as a doctor in this town—or anywhere in the South, for that matter—you'll have to find a way to fortify yourself against negro devilry. People are talking about you, you and your mulatto mistress, living together in this house, peddling her mama's superstitious backwoods spells and potions."

"That's nonsense," I replied, "and you know it."

"It's unbecoming of a civilized white man in your position. You'd do better to set up accommodations for your *placée*, if that's what she is. Give her a love nest suited to her kind over on Rampart Street. And please—for your own good and hers—" He paused, then placed a finger against my lips. "Never say Arabella's name again."

With that, he turned on his heel and stepped outside to join Williams on the street. As the door swung shut, I exhaled.

I had said what I must and heard what I must. Now I knew with utter clarity that I must do what I must and finish what I had begun.

The following evening, we celebrated a profitable week with a dinner of roast chicken, potatoes, carrots, and leeks, all washed down with a few bottles of good Italian wine. We were in high spirits, buoyed by laughter and the shared effort to cast a more hopeful light on the macabre events life had thrown our way during this strange and harrowing epidemic.

In that spirit, we even managed to speak about Arabella without lapsing into melancholy. We toasted her health, the health of her child, and a future where that child might grow up free, in a world where slavery had been crushed into oblivion.

During this pleasant interlude, I turned to Charlotte. "Have you ever thought about having children someday?"

She looked me over with a wry smile. "Why? You offering?"

"I just wondered how you imagined your future, and whether it included being a mother. I know you'd be splendid at it."

She shrugged. "Depends on what happens with this place. If I get my share, my future looks one way. If not, it looks another."

"How does it look now?"

"I can't work here forever, selling nasty poisons to gullible white folks."

"I see."

"It doesn't look like me standing behind that counter until the year 1900."

"So, no interest in raising children, then?"

She tilted her head. "I honestly can't tell if you're trying to court me right now."

A flush rose to my cheeks. "I'm not trying to court you."

"Thank the Lord for small mercies," she said, laughing.

I turned to Jerome. "What about you? Have you thought of having children someday?"

"Not really, Doc. Guess I'd have to find myself a husband first."

"You mean wife."

"Right. Wife."

"With your cooking skills, you'd make someone a wonderful husband. And I'm sure you'd make an excellent father, too."

Jerome nodded. "Thank you."

"Now I think he's trying to court you, Jerome," Charlotte said.

We laughed and sipped our wine.

"This is the best chicken I've ever had," I said. There was always something elusive, some bewitching flavor, in Jerome's cooking. "Would you care are to share any of your culinary secrets?"

He shook his head. "No secrets, Doc. Just good, fresh ingredients."

I turned back to Charlotte. "So, what'll you do with your share from the sale, if things go your way?"

"I don't know. Maybe rent my mother's old apartment, if it's still available."

"And if Sarah's lawyers succeed in stealing it from you?"

"Then I'll go to the ball, find myself a rich man, and start over."

She said it playfully, but I suspected there was some truth to it.

"But what will you do with your life?" I asked.

"I'll do what I always did. Run a shop. Work for Marie Laveau."

"What about you, Doc?" Jerome asked. "What'll you do if they sell this place?"

"I'll always be a doctor, I know that much. I was born to it."

"It's comforting, isn't it?" Charlotte said. "Believing in something? Doctoring. Big black books."

"Mercurous chloride," Jerome added. "Leeches."

"Indeed, it is," I replied, warmed by the wine and their company, and willing to ignore their ridicule.

"It's your religion," she said. "Your voodoo."

"Far from it. It's science. A bright, sweet peach in the dark forest of superstition."

We laughed again.

Charlotte raised her glass, peering into it. "This must be some strong wine."

"As for religion," I said, "its days are numbered. It's a toadstool growing in the darkness of ignorance."

"There are plenty of toadstools that grow in the light, too," Charlotte said. "And perfectly good mushrooms that grow in the dark."

She refilled our glasses from the third bottle.

"Only the poisonous ones grow in darkness," I said.

"Hiram," Charlotte said—thrilling me with her use of my given name—"you know even less about mushrooms than you know about people."

I smiled and nodded. I knew she was probably right.

And with that, the sadness that lingered like a persistent fog, and which no amount of Italian wine or Peruvian cocaine could dispel, settled once more over my heart.

Yet it was this very sense of having so little left to lose that steeled me to carry on with my plan.

24

I set down my glass of wine.

"Jerome, I've been meaning to ask you something."

"What is it?"

"It's about your sister."

"What about her?"

"Do you know how McFarland handles childbirths for his slaves? Does he attend to them himself?"

"Why do you want to know?"

"Call it... professional curiosity."

"You're not a midwife. Professionally."

"Then call it personal curiosity. Call it whatever you want. I'm concerned for your sister's well-being, that's all."

He sized me up for a moment, as if deciding whether to trust me with information pertaining to his sister.

"He uses a root doctor, Miss Mae. She's been his midwife for twenty years."

"J.W. McFarland uses a root doctor?"

"He's relied on her ever since one of his favorite girls died giving birth under his care. After that, he had Miss Mae take over. She's delivered thirty or so babies for him

since then, either at his house or down on his sugar planta-
tion."

"Thirty?"

"Something like that."

"Do you think you could arrange a meeting between her
and me?"

He scrutinized me. "Are you going to ask her to let my
sister's baby die?"

I held his gaze, then looked away. He took this to mean
yes.

"She won't do that," he said. "If Arabella wanted a dead
baby, she wouldn't need your help."

"You said she wouldn't kill it. But losing it during childbirth isn't the same as swallowing poison or throwing herself down the stairs."

"If it's on purpose, it's the same to her."

"I'm not suggesting anyone let the baby die on purpose.
I'm a doctor first. Do no harm. It's the Hippocratic Oath. I
stand by it."

"Oh, that's hypocritic, all right."

"Funny."

"And true."

I decided it was time to tell Jerome and Charlotte what
I'd been thinking.

After I'd done so, they informed me I'd lost my mind.

Then Jerome agreed to arrange a meeting between Mae
and me right away.

* * *

I arrived at Mae's house late the next morning. It was a modest wooden structure with ivy climbing the walls and orange and red flowers spilling from clay pots lining the porch.

I knocked. After a moment, the door creaked open to reveal a slender woman in her sixties, with deep lines etched in her face. Her hair was wrapped in a green scarf. She wore a simple brown dress.

"Doc Whitaker?"

"Yes, ma'am. You must be Miss Mae."

"Jerome said you be comin'."

"Thank you for seeing me on such short notice, Miss Mae."

She stepped aside. "Let's get this over with."

I entered the little house. A wooden table stood in the center of the front room, cluttered with dried plants, roots, and implements.

"You sit there," she said, pointing to a chair.

I sat, and she took a chair across from me.

"What you want to talk about?" she asked. "I don't chit-chat much with white folk."

"I don't chit-chat much with anyone," I replied.

"Well, get to it."

I felt nervous in her presence but tried to project an air of professional confidence. "Jerome tells me you use roots. To help ensure a safe birth."

She crossed her arms. "I do. That all?"

"Do you mind if I ask you what roots you use?"

"Ask all you want. I ain't tellin'."

"Trade secrets."

"Whatever. Root magic ain't for you. Don't work on whites, for some mysterious reason pertaining to not having a soul."

"You've never assisted a white birth?"

"Nope. That why you here? Worried about some white woman?"

"Professional curiosity, that's all. From one doctor to another."

"Then what did you want? Besides satisfyin' you white man-ical curiosity?"

"May I ask how many deliveries you've attended, Miss Mae?"

"Thousand. Two thousand. Something like that."

I leaned back, startled by the number. "And of those two thousand, how many would you say you've lost?"

"What you mean, lost?"

"How many babies or mothers have died? It must be quite a few."

"None. Never lost a mother or a baby."

Such a claim was impossible.

"At least one of every ten babies die," I said.

"None of mine ever did. Maybe they died later. Out in the field, or the back room. I can't watch over my babies or my mamas they whole life, though I wish I could. But when the baby comin' out, and the days after? Ain't none died."

"I see," I said, unsure whether to believe her.

"That all?"

"There is one other thing I wanted to ask."

"Ask it, then. Ain't got all day." She stared at me impatiently.

I considered leaving, but thought better of it. "I wonder if you'd ever pretend to lose a child?"

Her eyes widened.

"For a very respectable fee, of course," I hastened to add.

"What you mean, pretend?"

"Giving it something to make it appear dead without really harming it. Just long enough for it to be taken away."

"Away from what?"

"Slavery."

She shook her head. "I won't do nothin' like that."

"The mother is a slave," I said. "She doesn't want to deliver the child into bondage, but into freedom."

"I have a reputation, Mr. Whatever-your-name-is. I ain't lost one child ever. If I pretend to lose one, only two things gone happen. I lose my reputation. But first, most likely, I lose my life. I swing up there, dancing in the air. And when I'm up there swingin', I point down at you. 'Come up here, mister white man, come join me in the dance.' And then you up here dancin' with me. We dancin' together."

The exotic aroma of crepe myrtle, sewage, and rotting flesh drifted through the apothecary's open door. The scent, unpleasant as it was, had grown almost comforting in its familiarity.

"What did she say?" Jerome asked.

"Miss Mae is more concerned with her reputation than doing the right thing," I replied.

"Imagine that," Charlotte said from behind the counter.

I stood near the doorway, gazing out at the street with my back to her. Even so, I could hear the smirk in her voice.

Her expressiveness was one of the things I liked most about her, even when she used it to challenge me, which was often.

I turned toward Jerome, who was grinding kola nuts on the counter beside the soda machine. "Do you know if Mc-Farland has ever used any midwives other than Mae? She can't have been the only one in twenty years."

He paused what he was doing. "Did it himself once, five or six years ago, when Miss Mae was down with the fever. Twin girls, if I recall. Both died. Mother died a few days later."

"Then suppose she fell ill again and couldn't be there when your sister went into labor? I doubt McFarland would want to do it himself if someone else were available. Not after losing all three last time."

"You're serious about this, aren't you?" Jerome said.

"I am."

"Then what if Miss Mae fell ill with what, exactly?"

"There must be any number of temporary ailments that could incapacitate her."

"What about all that 'do no harm' stuff?"

"I don't intend to harm anyone. I merely wondered if it's possible for her to become unavailable for a while."

Jerome released the kola nut he was working on. It rolled across the counter, fell to the floor, and clattered into the shadows.

"Why are you so eager to help my sister?" he said.

They both watched me, waiting for my answer.

"I'm obliged by God's absence."

Charlotte shook her head. "Hiram, you are, *sans doute*, the craziest white man in New Orleans. I hope you know that."

She stepped out from behind the counter and embraced me, resting her head against my chest. "God isn't absent, my darling Hiram. He's very busy, that's all. Give Him a chance to do the right thing, and I promise you, He will. You're precious to Him. And to me."

If I didn't believe in her God, I believed in Charlotte. And, sometimes, I felt as if she believed in me, too. And that made all the difference in the world. Once, I might have demanded to know just how much time her God needed. Now, I let it be.

Charlotte returned to the counter and resumed preparing pills. "We could make Miss Mae sick for a while," she said, not looking up. "But it would be a lot easier if we could get her to go along with it. I'll go talk to her."

Later that day, Charlotte found Jerome and me in the courtyard, having coffee after a messy boil lancing.

"She'll do it," she said.

As she spoke, a few rays of sunlight broke through the clouds rushing by overhead. The petals and leaves strewn across the cobblestones glowed briefly before the sun disappeared again.

Jerome, seated on the bench by the fountain, leaned forward, pressing his hands against his thighs. "Then who's going to take care of my sister?"

"A woman named Claire," Charlotte said. "She did a delivery for McFarland a few years back, when Miss Mae was sick."

"How did you convince her to go along with it?" I asked.

"I offered her ten percent of my share of the house."

I caught my breath. That was a significant sum. "That's very generous of you," I said, though the words hardly conveyed what I felt.

Charlotte shrugged and smiled. "The Good Lord giveth, the Good Lord taketh away."

"Does she know it might be ten percent of nothing?" Jerome asked.

"I explained everything to her," Charlotte said.

"And she still went along with it?"

"She did."

"I guess she's not so afraid of dancing up there in the sky with me, after all," I said.

"I told her what a good dance partner you are."

I nodded.

Charlotte looked at me for a moment. I couldn't read her expression.

"What?" I said.

"When I was leaving, she said, 'I hope you're not too attached to that white man of yours.' I asked her what she meant, and she said, 'He ain't long for this God's green earth.'"

Jerome rubbed his hands together, as if warding off a sudden chill. "Hopefully she's a worse fortune-teller than she is a midwife."

25

The following day, I returned from a visit to the cigar factory to find Jerome upstairs tending to Jeremiah Forsythe, a middle-aged man with a badly broken foot. He'd gotten it stuck in the trolley tracks on Canal Street and been subsequently run over by a horse that had thrown its rider. Jerome had already administered morphine and was carefully cleaning the injury.

"Doesn't look good, Doc," Jerome said as I pulled up a stool to the surgery table where Forsythe lay groaning.

I had to agree. The ankle was broken clean through and the foot was twisted at an obscene angle. The ripped tissue, torn tendons, and severed nerves appeared beyond repair.

"I don't think we can set this, Mr. Forsythe," I said.

"You got to," Forsythe whimpered. "I can't be no cripple. I carry things for a living. That's all I know how to do. You gotta fix it."

Jerome and I exchanged a glance at this fortuitous opportunity.

"What do you think?" I asked him.

"We could try to set it, but I don't—"

"You gotta set it!" Forsythe yelped. Then, nearly a whisper: "I can't be no cripple. I have to provide."

"Charlotte could probably fix it," I said, testing the waters.

"Charlotte? Who's that?"

"Our front counter woman," Jerome said.

"She has certain talents," I added.

"Talents? What talents?"

"She uses voodoo spells to heal folks," Jerome said. "Good at it, too. But we don't do voodoo here at Whitaker's."

Forsythe's eyes lit up. "Get that voodoo princess up here right now! Get her up here to do her black magic!"

"Really, I think we should just lop it off," I said.

"No! Get the girl. Get her up here!"

"Mr. Forsythe," Jerome said, "Miss France is not—"

"Get her," I said. "Mr. Forsythe is right. Miss France is his only hope."

Jerome went downstairs and soon came back with Charlotte.

"He wants you to use your magic," I told her. "Isn't that right, Mr. Forsythe?"

"That's right," Forsythe said. "Do whatever you gotta do, Miss Charlotte. I know you can help me."

"I'll do what I can, Mr. Forsythe."

I pulled back the towel covering the loosely-connected foot.

Charlotte inhaled and placed a hand on his shoulder. "I'm no doctor, Mr. Forsythe. Are you sure you don't want Doctor Whitaker to try to fix it?"

"No, ma'am. He'll just lop it off."

"If Jerome and I do our best to set the bone," I said, "can you improve his chances of keeping the foot?"

She glanced at the mangled limb. "I can try."

"You gotta do it," Forsythe pleaded. "I can't be no cripple."

"Do what you can," Charlotte said. "I'll be back."

With that, she left the surgery and ascended to the third floor.

Jerome and I began our work, cutting away what couldn't be saved, stitching veins, arteries, and nerves, reconnecting the foot as best we could. When we were finished, Jerome went upstairs and returned with Charlotte, who carried several bags of supplies which she laid out on the counter.

From the first bag she withdrew a carved wooden pendant, a candle, and a rosary. From the second she took a mortar and pestle, along with roots, powders, and herbs—I recognized mandrake and belladonna among them—which she dropped into the mortar. She uncorked a small brown bottle and sprinkled a rose-scented liquid over the mixture, then clipped a lock of Forsythe's hair and trimmed his fingernails, adding them in. She wiped blood from his wound and dropped the bloodied cloth into the mortar, followed by a few pieces of dried lizard's tail, and a pinch of snake scales from a purple velvet pouch.

She lit a stick of incense, then murmured a prayer as she ground the ingredients into a thick, sweet-yet-foul-smelling paste:

"Blessed Mother Mary, help me heal and protect this soul in need. Spirits, ancestors, lend me your grace. Bless our work today."

Jerome left the room and returned with a tea set. Charlotte scooped a spoonful of the mixture into the teapot and stirred it with a silver spoon.

"Let it steep for two minutes," she said. "Then strain it and fill a syringe. Inject it into his *derrière*."

We waited in silence as the mixture steeped, then prepared the dose. When the time came, Jerome turned Forsythe onto his side, and I administered the injection. He winced once, then let out a soft breath. Jerome adjusted his pillow and tucked the blanket around him, while Charlotte gently closed his eyes with her palm.

"You'll sleep now," she said. "When you wake, you'll already have begun to heal."

"Yes, ma'am," Forsythe whispered. His body relaxed, and he drifted off.

Charlotte clasped her hands, closed her eyes, and spoke another prayer: "Oshun, goddess of sweet water, bring your calming touch. Raphael, archangel of healing, surround us with light. Through the power of the Father, the Son, and the Holy Spirit, restore this man's health and strength. Bondye, supreme creator, bless us. Faith and spirit, work through us. Fill this room with healing and love. We place our trust in your divine will."

I placed my hand to Forsythe's mouth; his breathing was slow and shallow. I opened his shirt, placed the stethoscope to his chest, and counted. "Forty... Thirty..."

His respiration rate was falling with each breath.

"Are you sure you got the dose right?" I asked.

"I mixed it exactly as Marie told me," Charlotte replied.

"And you're certain she never lost anyone with this... trick?"

"I didn't ask."

I checked again and felt only the faintest exhalation. My stomach lurched.

"What if we're killing a man who came in with a broken foot?"

"Most men with feet this broken die anyway," Jerome said.

I listened for Forsythe's heartbeat again.

Nothing.

A full minute passed.

Still nothing.

My insides sank. No man could live without a beating heart.

Ka-thunk—his heart jolted.

Mine did too.

I adjusted the stethoscope's diaphragm and counted.

Ka-thunk. Ten seconds between beats.

Please let this man live.

Thunk thunk. Eight seconds.

Duhn-duhn. Six.

He was reviving.

"He's coming back," I said, my voice trembling.

"Damn it," Charlotte muttered.

"He's going to live," I said.

"Of course he's going to live," she snapped.

"What are we going to do?" Jerome asked. "He was supposed to stay dead for at least an hour."

"I didn't adjust the dose for a grown man," Charlotte said. "That's it. It must be."

26

The icebox was a wooden cabinet with a varnished oak exterior, standing in the corner of the apothecary opposite the soda fountain. If one stood close enough, he could hear the soft trickle of meltwater dripping through the drainage hole into the pan below. As far as I knew, we were the only apothecary in New Orleans fortunate enough to own such a modern appliance.

With Charlotte and Jerome standing behind me, I reached for the brass handle, grasped it, and paused, sensing, in some mystical way, that I was about to open something far greater than an icebox door. It was, rather, a portal into another life I couldn't envision, yet one I had already chosen.

I pulled the handle. The latch clanked, released, the door gave way, and a dry coolness spilled out around the edges. As I swung the door open, its hinges resisted with a low, whispered creak.

The interior of the icebox was divided into two compartments. The upper one held a large block of ice, delivered just this morning. The lower held various perishables —vials of smallpox vaccine, tinctures of digitalis, jars of mercury compounds, silver nitrate solutions, and cod liver oil.

Jerome and Charlotte peered into the cool interior but saw only a large block of ice.

"What are we supposed to see?" Jerome said.

I slid my hands behind the forty-pound block, pulled it out, braced it against my chest, and carried it to the counter. When I returned, Charlotte and Jerome were staring into the icebox, at a burlap bundle that had been hidden behind the ice block.

"Is that...?" Charlotte said, the words trailing off.

I reached in, took the bundle from the compartment, and placed it on the counter, where I unwrapped it to reveal a small, six-pound, eight-ounce black baby, curled up as though it were merely sleeping, beautiful even in its frozen state.

"Where did you get that?" Charlotte whispered.

"From a dead woman in the cathedral gardens," I replied. "Napoleon led me to her."

Jerome stepped back. "We're going to hang for this."

Alex and Gigi Johnson, the parents of Danielle, the girl I'd lost to yellow fever, lived in a two-room shack at the edge of a dusty, weed-strewn clearing on the east side of the Quarter. It was twilight when I arrived. Fireflies flickered in the mulberry bushes, and the first stars had begun to show. A crescent moon hung low in the western sky.

At the door, Mr. Johnson and I exchanged brief greetings. I asked if I might come in to speak with him and Mrs.

Johnson. He hesitated, his hands pressed against the door-frame, then stepped aside.

The front room was spare and tidy: a worn-out settee sagged against one wall, a chipped table sat beside it. A few framed drawings, faded and slightly askew, adorned the walls.

Mr. Johnson gestured toward the settee. I took a seat.

"Gigi," he called to the back room, "Doctor Whitaker's here. Wants to talk to us about something."

A moment later, Gigi Johnson appeared, wearing a plain black dress and blue apron, drying her hands on a dishrag.

I stood. "Good evening, Mrs. Johnson. Here, why don't you—"

"You sit," Mr. Johnson said. "Gigi's fine standing."

"Please," I said, gesturing toward the settee.

"I'm fine standing," she said softly, her eyes never quite meeting mine.

I nodded and sat again. Mrs. Johnson remained by the rear door, twisting the dishrag between her fingers, her gaze fixed somewhere to my left.

"If you came to check on my wife," Mr. Johnson said, "there's no need. She was laid up for a few days, but she's back on her feet now."

"I'm glad to hear that," I replied.

They both nodded, but offered nothing more.

"I want you to know how sorry I am for your loss," I said.

Neither responded.

"I've lost loved ones, too," I said. "So I have some idea of how it feels. In fact, my own sister—"

"If that's all, Doctor," Mrs. Johnson cut in, her voice sad and bitter, "I have chores to attend to. I don't need to hear about your sister."

"Of course," I replied quickly. "I'm sorry. Actually, there was something else I wanted to talk about."

Her eyes found mine and searched my face. "What is it?"

"This may sound unusual," I said, "but suppose another child was born—another black child—and its mother died during childbirth. With no father or other family to look after it…"

"Yes? What about it?" she said.

"I wonder if you would consider taking that child in as your own."

"You mean as a replacement for Danielle?" Mr. Johnson said.

"No," I said quickly, shaking my head. "No one could possibly replace Danielle. But if there was a newborn in desperate need of a loving home, I couldn't think of a better family to care for it than your own."

Mr. Johnson shook his head. "I don't think so."

"Yes," Mrs. Johnson said. "Yes. I want that baby. If you got another baby that needs mothering, I want it. I want to mother that baby."

The midwives, Mae and Claire, came to finalize the details of the scheme. We met in the courtyard.

Claire, it turned out, wanted the same ten percent of Charlotte's share as Mae had been offered, but in cash, up front, claiming she was taking the biggest risk. She'd asked around and learned the townhouse might fetch ten thousand dollars or more. If Charlotte's cut was $2,500, Claire wanted $250.

It was a lot, and now we'd have to pay it twice. Still, it seemed a small price to pay for a life of freedom, even someone else's. To my surprise, Jerome agreed to pay Claire from his own funds.

With that settled, Claire said, "Let's see this dead baby in the icebox."

I retrieved it, laid it on the bench, and carefully unwrapped it.

"Yep, that's a dead baby, all right," Claire said. "You better thaw it out before Arabella's ready to pop. McFarland ain't dumb enough to believe his girl birthed no frozen baby."

We stared at the tiny, lifeless form.

"Mighty cute for a frozen little dead thing, though," Claire said.

We murmured our agreement.

"What happened to the mama? You kill her?"

"Died of yellow fever."

"Where's her body at?"

"Where she died. In the bushes behind the cathedral."

Claire frowned. "When was that?"

"A few days ago."

"They're gonna smell her if they didn't already—dead folk stink."

"I've been reading the papers," I said. "There's been no mention of a dead woman with her belly cut open. I covered her stomach with her dress. My hope is they won't notice."

"Just toss her on the big stack of dead black folk like another piece of firewood on the pile, right?" Claire said.

"Something like that."

"Why you want me to do this thing, anyway? I'm glad for the money, but it's a big risk for everybody. Especially me."

"Because," Jerome said, "I don't want my sister's child to be a slave."

It was the first time I'd heard him voice that sentiment. I'd long since convinced myself of the moral necessity of my plan, yet I couldn't help but wonder if I had fallen under some kind of spell, and whether Jerome had now fallen under it too.

Claire folded her arms. "So Miss Mae's gonna get word that Arabella gone into labor, then y'all are gonna give her the Make-Sick potion."

"I'll take it to her," Charlotte said.

"Then someone from McFarland gonna come and tell me Miss Mae can't do the birthin' because she's laid up. 'I'm real busy right now,' I say, 'but all right, I'll come and do it.'"

I nodded.

"So I pack my basket with supplies, but in the bottom there's this dead baby under the blankets, who better be good and thawed."

"I'll be sure it's ready," I said.

"So I go to Arabella's room. If McFarland's not there, and no one's watching, I deliver the baby, inject it with some of these Pretend-Dead drops to keep it quiet, and switch it for the real dead one. Then I say, 'Oh no, this poor child born dead.' That about it?"

"Yes," Charlotte and I said together.

"But even if someone's watching," I added, "you can still make the switch later and say the baby died afterward."

Claire nodded. "Yeah, if the baby looks the same and if it's got a little boy thing on it."

"Right," I said.

"Claire'll need to stay and attend to Arabella for several hours, maybe even days," Mae said. "We can't have that live baby hiding in the basket that long. How we getting it out to the people who gone take care of it?"

"There's a back gate to the courtyard," Jerome said. "It unlocks from the inside. She can bring the basket there in the middle of the night, and I'll take it."

"No," I said. "I'll take it."

They looked at me in surprise.

"Of course it has to be me," I said. "I'll deliver the child to the Johnsons. They don't need to know anyone else is involved. If anything goes wrong, I'll take the blame. Jerome, I know she's your sister, but you can't be involved."

"But I can be?" Claire said.

"I don't see any other way. And we're paying you fairly."

Claire sighed. "All right," she said, with a slow nod.

Then we all fell silent, whether in prayer or contemplation of what lay ahead.

DIABOLICAL MURDER SHOCKS NEW ORLEANS! BODY FOUND BEHIND CATHEDRAL! declared the *Pelican*.

CATHEDRAL BUTCHER STRIKES! GRISLY SCENE DISCOVERED IN THE QUARTER, read the *Delta*.

NEW ORLEANS' OWN FIEND! MURDER BEHIND CATHEDRAL ECHOES HARPE BROTHERS' BRUTALITY, CITY LAID LOW SINKS FURTHER STILL, announced the *Picayune*.

It was the morning after our meeting. Noticing the headlines in a news stand, I bought copies of all three papers and read them on the balcony.

The thrust of each article was the same: an unidentified black woman had been found murdered behind the cathedral. "In what can only be described as a satanic voodoo ritual," the *Pelican* reported, the woman had been cut open and robbed of her full-term fetus. The *Picayune* described the scene as one of "unfathomable barbarity," likening it to the worst atrocities of the Harpe Brothers, who had murdered and mutilated their way across the South in the 1790s. The word *voodoo* appeared in ominous italics, as though the murder's alleged connection to dark magic heightened the horror.

The Chief of Police pledged swift justice, declaring that capturing and hanging the fiend responsible—"likely a large negro male"—was now the department's top priority. He assured the public that all available resources would be devoted to solving the crime.

As I read, Napoleon jumped up onto the table and inserted himself between me and the newspaper, as if to stop me from reading further.

"What have you got me into, little cat?" I asked him, as he rubbed himself against my arm.

Later, I discussed the situation with Charlotte and Jerome before opening up shop. Both were of the comforting opinion that—given the victim's race and gender—the chief's vow to use "all available resources" would amount to "no resources at all."

Later that morning, word arrived that Arabella had gone into labor.

The dead baby had spent the night in the lower compartment of the icebox rather than behind the ice block, so it was as ready as it would ever be to play its part in freeing Arabella's live child.

27

A carriage waited outside Mae's house, ready to take her to the McFarland estate. In the kitchen, Mae stirred the Make-Sick potion Charlotte had given her, then lit a special candle, filling the room with aromatic smoke. She closed her eyes and recited the prayer Charlotte had helped her memorize: "Spirits, ancestors, guide me, protect me. Let my body rest, but ensure my health. Guardian loa, watch over me. Saint Michael, defend me. Holy Mother full of grace, bring me back to—"

"What're you doing?" one of the carriage men said from the kitchen doorway, having entered the house uninvited.

Mae opened her eyes. "Saying a prayer for the master's baby."

"Get a move on, then. No time for that."

"Go outside. I'll be out in a minute."

He hesitated. She waved him away.

"More than a minute, I'll come drag you out," he said, before stepping outside.

Mae finished the prayer, swallowed the potion, and went out to the carriage.

As it bumped and swayed through the city's rutted streets, Mae began to worry. Had she mixed the potion correctly? If it failed, she'd have no choice but to deliver Arabella's baby and hand it over to McFarland. But before they crossed Canal Street, the symptoms struck. Her stomach lurched, she convulsed, doubled over, and vomited. Blood dripped from her nose.

Struggling to speak, she managed: "Take me to Doctor Whitaker's on Chartres. Fetch Claire Dubois on Burgundy. She delivered his babies before." Then she collapsed.

Instead of bringing her to my practice, the carriage men dumped Mae on the banquette at Bourbon and Canal streets, believing her already dead. She would lie there for hours, stepped over by passersby, before finally coming to.

Meanwhile, I'd received word the plot was underway. I delivered the "package" to Claire, and soon after, McFarland's men arrived to take her to the estate.

They reached McFarland's around three in the afternoon. Susan, a young house servant, greeted them and led Claire to the slave quarters. There, Arabella lay in bed, drenched in sweat and breathing hard. Judith, another servant, stood nearby.

There was no sign of J.W. McFarland.

"You want me to stay?" Judith asked.

"No, we're better off by ourselves," Claire said. "Go on now. I'll call if I need you."

Once Judith left, Claire pulled a small table close to the bed and lit a stick of incense. Raising her voice slightly for the benefit of any eavesdroppers, she said, "My name's Claire, Miss Arabella. Miss Mae took ill. I'm gonna help you instead." She set the basket down and began arranging her supplies. "Everything gonna be fine, don't you worry." She moved closer to the bed. "I done a few births for Mr. McFarland before. You and this baby gonna be fine. This is the easy part. That baby gonna pop right out, healthy as a buttered biscuit."

"Thank you," Arabella groaned.

Claire moved to Arabella's side and gently pressed her abdomen to assess the baby's position and the strength of the contractions. "Yep, we gonna have us a baby, all right," she said. She offered Arabella a sip of water and pressed a cool cloth to her forehead.

As her labor intensified, Arabella's moans deepened.

Twice, other servants peeked in, but Claire waved them off. "Leave us be. She's doing good. You're just bothering us."

"My back hurts," Arabella groaned through gritted teeth, "down through my legs."

"That's all right, Miss Arabella. You just keep breathing like I showed you. In through your nose, out through your mouth. You're doin' real good."

By ten o'clock Arabella was trembling, her back pains worsening, and her moans growing louder.

"You doing fine. We almost there now," Claire said. "Push when you feel it tryin' to get out."

Arabella bore down with all her strength, her face contorted in agony. The contractions came fast—one a minute. She cursed.

"Any minute now," Claire said.

Half an hour passed.

"Let's get you up to a squat, help the baby fall out," Claire said, guiding her into position.

"Urnggh," Arabella cried. "Oh God, it's coming. I can feel it."

"Good. Now down on your behind, knees up. That's it," Claire said, helping her.

Arabella leaned back into the pillows. The baby's head began to emerge.

"Oh my," Claire said. She reached for the baby. "Oh my," she repeated.

"What?" Arabella gasped. "What is it?"

"Something funny 'bout this baby," Claire said.

"Funny? What do you mean, funny?"

"You got a head of curls coming out of you. Bright, shiny, red ones."

"Oh, God," Arabella moaned.

"One more push," Claire urged.

Arabella pushed hard and let out a sharp cry. The baby fell into Claire's hands.

"And your baby white," Claire said.

"Shit," said a voice behind her.

Claire turned. McFarland stood in the doorway.

"Let me see my baby," Arabella said.

Claire began clearing the baby's airway.

McFarland stepped in and shut the door behind him. "Is he healthy?"

"It's a boy? Let me see him," Arabella demanded, struggling to sit up.

"Yeah, it's a boy all right," Claire replied, her eyes locked on McFarland's.

"Finish up and give him to me," McFarland said. Then, to Arabella: "You don't need to see it, girl."

"Give him to me!" she cried.

Claire picked up the scissors.

McFarland raised a hand. "Put those down, Claire."

She ignored him, cut the cord, tied it off with a length of twine, then placed the baby on Arabella's breast. "Make sure he gets a good suck."

"Oh God, he's beautiful," Arabella whispered as she stroked the baby's red curls. "He looks exactly like his daddy."

Claire turned to McFarland. "What're you gonna do with him?"

"None of your business, Claire."

"And your missus? What's she supposed to think?"

"If Mrs. McFarland hears a word about this—from you or from anyone—I'll have you whipped dead like a dog." He looked at Arabella. "That goes for you too, girl."

He stepped forward to take the baby, but Arabella clung to it and swatted at McFarland's face, slicing his cheek with a fingernail.

"No!" she shrieked. "Leave him alone! Leave my baby be!"

"Hold on," Claire said.

McFarland stepped back.

"I can help you," Claire said. "Nobody needs to get hurt, and your missus don't need to learn nothin'."

"What are you proposing?" McFarland replied.

"Lot of folks lost children to the fever. I know a family lost their boy. They'd take this one, no questions asked. Give him a good life."

"You can't take him from me," Arabella wailed.

"You have no say in this," McFarland snapped.

"Arabella, listen to me," Claire said. "You want your baby smothered with a pillow and tossed down the well? Or you want him to live free?"

"I don't intend to toss it down the well," McFarland said. "I intend to bury it among white, Christian people."

"No!" Arabella screamed, tears streaming down her face.

"Mr. McFarland," Claire said, "I know you gotta 'count for this baby. Whole house knows Arabella been pregnant, you can't hide that. But I got a way to make this work for everybody."

McFarland sighed. "For the love of God, girl, spit it out."

Claire went to the basket, removed the blankets, hesitated, then lifted out the bundle and laid it on the table.

"What is it?" McFarland asked, stepping between Arabella and the table.

"What you got over there?" Arabella said.

Claire unwrapped the bundle.

"What in hell is that?" McFarland said.

"Died a few days ago. Mother pulled through, thank you Jesus, but this little one didn't make it."

"How tragic," McFarland said flatly. "So what's this about?"

"How 'bout we trade this one for that one?" Claire said.

McFarland seemed to consider it.

"That way you got something to bury," Claire continued. "Something to show your missus. Something to show the others. You got your story, baby gets its life."

"And you've been carrying this dead baby around for how long?"

"What dead baby?" Arabella said.

"Two or three days," Claire said. "Lost count."

McFarland examined the tiny body more closely. "Remarkable condition for having been dead several days."

"Some of them stay fresh a while. Take they time to turn."

"And you felt you should bring it along for Arabella's birth."

"Only found out I was coming here just before, on account of Miss Mae fallin' ill. Had it with me already."

He pinched the dead baby's thigh. "My drivers mentioned Mae asking them to take her to Hiram Whitaker's place when she fell ill."

Claire stared at him. "Hiram what now? Who that?"

"Doctor Whitaker, over on Chartres Street."

Claire shook her head. "I don't know no Doctor Whitaker."

"His slave boy, by coincidence, happens to be Arabella's brother."

"I don't know nothin' 'bout that."

"Did you know Arabella tried to kill herself rather than give birth to another slave?"

"I don't—"

"Now look at her, clinging to that little white thing like it's the most precious gift in the world."

Claire glanced at the baby on Arabella's breast. "It is cute, with them curls and all."

"What was the plan, Claire, after you swapped this black corpse for Arabella's baby? Were you going to sell it? Or was her brother going to raise it as his own?"

Claire shook her head. "Wasn't no plan like that."

"How did you intend to abscond with Arabella's child? That's what I fail to understand. What if it cried out from the bottom of the basket when you tried to leave?"

"You know what, Mr. McFarland? I'm just gonna go now, take my dead baby with me. You do whatever you want with that live one. I did my job."

She moved to wrap up the dead baby.

McFarland placed his hand on hers. "You're not going anywhere, Claire. You'll stay right here and tell us who put you up to this when the police arrive." He released her hand, stepped out of the room, and locked the door.

"Damn it!" Claire said. "Damn it, damn it, damn it."

I arrived at the rear door to McFarland's courtyard at 3 a.m., waited five minutes, then knocked softly.

"Doctor Whitaker?" came Claire's whisper.

"Yes. It's me."

The latch clicked, and the door opened a few inches. Claire peered out.

"Come in," she said.

I hesitated. That wasn't part of the plan. She was supposed to hand me the basket with the live baby and I'd vanish into the night with it. There was no reason for me to enter the courtyard. A warning stirred in my gut, but I ignored my instincts and stepped inside.

The basket sat on the ground beside her.

"How did it go?" I asked.

"It went all right. Mother and baby both fine."

"Good," I said, reaching for the basket. "I should take it now before—"

"There's just a small problem, Doctor Whitaker," Claire said.

"Problem?"

"I'm truly sorry."

28

"The baby's white," Claire said. "Look for yourself."

"Damn it." I knelt beside the basket and peeled back the blankets. The moonlight revealed the dead black baby I'd cut from the woman's womb behind the cathedral. I looked up at Claire. "What is this? You were supposed to switch it for the live one."

Before she could answer, several men emerged from the trees. Two of them leveled shotguns at my chest.

"What—" I stammered.

"I'm so sorry, Doctor Whitaker," Claire said again. "I really am."

"Well, if it isn't the baby-stealing fiend of the cathedral gardens," McFarland said, the words seeming to emanate from the barrel of the shotgun braced against his shoulder.

"I had to tell them everything," Claire said. "Or they were gonna toss me down the well."

"Stand up, Whicket," McFarland said.

I stood, raising my hands over my head. I'd never stared down the barrel of a gun before, and I found it terrifying—that I could cease to be at the twitch of another man's finger.

There was so much I'd left undone in this life.

"Hands down, Whicket."

I lowered them and tried to focus on the other men present. The one on the left bore a striking resemblance to J.W. McFarland—same red curls, pockmarked face, hard gray eyes that glinted in the moonlight like steel. The one on the right was short and round, his eyes shaded beneath the brim of a police captain's cap. A gun belt hung from his hips, the pistols' pearl-inlaid grips sparkling in the moonlight as brightly as the bubbles in Charlotte's champagne.

Charlotte. How I'll miss you when I'm gone.

"Your girl here told us how your slave boy convinced you to steal his sister's baby," the police captain said.

"I didn't say nothin' like that," Claire said.

"And how your voodoo princess brewed up this here magic potion," he said, holding up the vial—"to keep the baby silent when she smuggled it off. How J.W.'s midwife Mae took part in the scheme to rob J.W.'s brother Finn here of his rightful property."

"What do you have to say to that, Whicket?" McFarland asked.

I'd barely heard the words. I was already whirling away through space in Charlotte's arms, far from this moonlit courtyard and the devils gathered here within it.

"Conspiracy to kidnap a child may or may not be a capital offense," McFarland said. "Captain Hotchkiss here says that's for the prosecutors to decide. As for me, I'm convinced that murdering a woman and slashing her belly open to steal her fetus is punishable by hanging."

My eyes drifted to a fourth figure cloaked in the shadows beneath the magnolia tree. It wasn't until the shape of his hat took form, the edges of its brim sketched by moonlight, that I knew it was Baron Sunday.

"Well, Whicket," McFarland said, "say something."

"None of them had anything to do with it," I said. "It was me and her." I nodded toward Claire. "If she said anything else, she's lying—trying to save herself by spreading the blame."

McFarland lowered his shotgun a hair. "You're a piece of work, Whicket. A genuine piece of work."

"It's Whitaker."

"I don't know how Jerome talked you into it. It's a revelation, really, what a white Northerner will do for a negro he barely knows."

"Jerome had nothing to do with this. Leave him out of it."

"The courts'll sort that out. Or more likely a lynch mob. But I'll tell you this: I'm not keen to see anyone get whipped nor strung up on account of you, whether it was your plan or theirs."

"It was mine," I said.

"And I don't want you thinking poorly of me," he said, "or believing I lack understanding or compassion."

"You are the least understanding, least compassionate man I have ever known."

"Be that as it may, like any man—any Southern man, at least—my most precious possession is my honor. And like any Southern man, I will not have my honor stolen, nor tolerate any attempt to steal it. Therefore, I am prepared to settle this as a matter of honor, not of laws. Captain Hotchkiss here has assured me of his blessing in this matter."

He's going to kill me right here.

I closed my eyes and tried to brace myself for the shotgun's blast, but couldn't imagine how to do it without cowering. Which I would not do, not in front of J.W. McFarland.

"What do you say, Hiram T. Whitaker? Honor, or law?"

What?

I opened my eyes. "I'm sorry, I don't—"

"I'm challenging you to a duel, you Northern shit-for-brains. Do you accept or don't you?"

Focus, Hiram.

"You're saying if we duel, you won't press charges against the others?"

"That's precisely what I'm saying, you idiot. Jesus Christ, Whicket, you are the slowest, least-witted man I have ever had the displeasure of knowing."

I tried to weigh the options logically. On the one hand, my co-conspirators and I, aided by a capable lawyer, might find mercy from a jury. On the other, a duel would almost certainly result in me being shot dead by J.W. McFarland.

Wait. We're talking about pistols, aren't we? Good God, what if he means to run me through with a sword?

Above us, someone lit a lamp on the veranda. Shadows in the distorted shapes of men spread across the courtyard.

Baron Sunday stepped from the darkness into the pool of light. He raised his right hand, formed the shape of a pistol, aimed it at McFarland's head, and pulled the trigger. "Bang," he said.

McFarland flinched and slapped at his neck. "Damnable mosquitoes," he muttered.

"Honor," I said. "I choose honor."

* * *

Captain Hotchkiss retained the dead baby as evidence and released Claire and me on our own recognizance. If I failed to appear at The Oaks dueling ground at the appointed hour, we would be apprehended and prosecuted "without mercy." Given my ignorance of guns and dueling, McFarland and his men granted me two days to prepare—to ensure an honorable outcome. The duel was set for ten o'clock on Saturday morning. If Jerome agreed to be my second, he'd meet McFarland's brother Finn the day before to finalize the details.

Finn asked Claire to stay the night to watch over Arabella, but she declined, preferring to be escorted home in McFarland's carriage. The driver warned her to stay there until "that business on Saturday is wrapped up."

I left on foot, arriving home at dawn to find Jerome and Charlotte awake, awaiting my return. I recounted everything that had happened as we sipped Jerome's coffee in the courtyard—nothing had ever tasted so good. And while my emotions swung wildly between terror and resignation, Charlotte and Jerome remained remarkably composed. Jerome volunteered to be my second before I even asked, and promised to retrieve a dueling pistol later that day to instruct me in its use.

"McFarland has killed six people that I know of," he said, "so you'll want to practice before Saturday."

"Six?"

"On the positive side, each shot was clean through the heart, so you won't need to suffer much."

"That's certainly comforting."

"Who's going to be your attending physician?" Charlotte asked.

The thought hadn't occurred to me. I assumed either McFarland or I would die, leaving the other unscathed. What need was there for an attending physician? But then her meaning dawned on me.

"I want you there," I said.

"That's not what I asked," she replied. "But all right. I know why you're doing this—you don't have a choice. But I don't want to watch you die, if I can do anything about it."

If I'm going to die, I want yours to be the last face I ever see, I thought. But "I'll try not to, then," was all I said.

In truth, I was terrified of dying. There was so much more life to live, even if I could no longer envision the precise contours of that life.

Charlotte placed a hand on mine. "I'm going to pray for you. And I'm going to cast two spells, whether you like it or not. One to keep your heart beating, and the other to stop McFarland's."

I slid my hand from beneath hers and rested it on top, giving it a light squeeze.

"Thank you, Charlotte."

"You're welcome, Hiram darling."

Jerome handed me the dueling pistol. I took it and felt its heft.

"Is it loaded?" I asked.

He shook his head. "I'll load it when the time comes. Hand it back. I'll show you how it works."

Eager to get rid of the loathsome thing, I handed it back.

Jerome picked up a small leather pouch with a brass spout. "Just before the duel, I'll charge the barrel with powder." He inserted the spout into the muzzle, tilted the gun back as if to pour powder into it, then set the pouch down. "Next, I cover the muzzle with a piece of linen and place the ball on it." He drew a wooden rod from beneath the barrel. "Then I drive it down with the ramrod." He mimed the motion. "Now," he said, "we cock the flint back and lock it."

"Hence, flintlock," I said.

"Right. Then I put a pinch of powder in the pan, right here. When you pull the trigger, the flint strikes—like this." He pulled the trigger, and the flint snapped down to strike the plate, sending a shower of sparks flying. "*Voilà*. The spark ignites the powder, the flame flashes through the vent"—he pointed to a tiny hole in the side of the barrel —"and sets off the charge, firing the ball."

He looked at me to see if I was following. I nodded, though the pounding in my chest had drowned out most of his words. The metallic tang of struck flint hung in the air.

"A lot has to happen between pulling the trigger and the ball leaving the barrel," he said.

I nodded. "Mm-hmm."

"That's why you have to hold your aim steady. Use your breath. It's only a second or two, but with your life on the line it'll feel like forever."

Is this how I'll die? I wondered. *Not in some grand, heroic act of saving lives, but from a lead ball fired by J.W. McFarland?*

I thought of all the lives I'd failed to save; mine, I realized, would just be the last name on a long list.

"I think I understand," I said quietly.

"Good. Now, if both of you miss, that might be the end of it. It depends on the arrangements I make with McFarland's second, his brother Finn."

"That would be a delightful outcome," I said. "Both of us missing."

"There's also a chance you'll have to reload and do it all over again. Sometimes there's a set number of tries before we call it a draw."

"And if one of us is too injured to continue?"

"That's usually the end of it."

"Usually?"

"Yes. Now, McFarland's going to have better pistols than this one—Wogdens, most likely. They'll weigh about the same, so we can practice with this one. But his'll have hair triggers. You cock 'em forward to increase the spring tension. Barely touch it, it fires. Rush it, and you waste your shot into the sky."

"You seem to know a lot about dueling."

"I was Mr. Dufilho's second a few times."

"He dueled?"

"Yes, sir."

"Who did he duel?"

"His patients."

"You're joking."

"People upset he couldn't cure their syphilis, mostly. Called him a charlatan. No doctor in New Orleans can let a slur like that go unanswered and stay in business."

"He survived, apparently."

"He didn't enjoy killing his patients, though. One news-paper ran a piece on it, back in '45. 'Local doctor fails to kill patient with leeches—succeeds with pistols.'"

I didn't know whether to laugh or cry. Lately, I didn't know what to feel about a lot of things. Even the prospect of my impending death at The Oaks left me torn. In some ways, it would simplify things—at least for me. And if, by the miraculous intervention of a God I didn't believe in, I succeeded in killing McFarland, who would sign off on my internship?

Later that day, Jerome returned from the McFarland es-tate, where he'd gone to settle the details with Finn.

"Seventeen paces," he said. "Counted out loud by me and Finn. Then turn and fire. We can practice in the court-yard."

"And if we both miss?" I asked, as I rinsed blood from a hacksaw in the sink.

"We reload."

"How many times?"

"Until one of you is dead."

29

A crisp breeze stirred the leaves overhead as Charlotte, Jerome, and I dismounted. We tied our horses to trees near the edge of the clearing and approached McFarland and his entourage, who were gathered around a small table. Upon it rested two dueling pistols in a black enamel case lined with red velvet.

"Looks like he's brought half the city," Jerome said, eyeing the cluster of men.

McFarland and I shook hands. He introduced me to his twin brother, Finn—whom I'd already met under equally unfortunate circumstances—and to Captain Hotchkiss, present to oversee the legalities of the duel's outcome.

Nearby stood McFarland's lawyer, R.W. Frederick, a slight man with beady eyes and a glued-on smirk; Dr. Samuel Pembroke, with a large satchel at his feet; and Father Malachy O'Reilly, McFarland's confessor from Saint Patrick's, with a large silver crucifix hanging from his neck.

"Gentlemen," I said, doing my best to mask my nauseating terror, "this is my medical assistant, Jerome—"

"Your slave, you mean," Captain Hotchkiss said dryly.

"And this," I continued, ignoring the captain's interruption, "is my attending physician, Miss Charlotte France."

McFarland's associates exchanged incredulous looks, then scoffed in unison.

For an instant, I regretted the slow reload of flintlocks, which prevented me from shooting the lot of them in the face before they knew what hit them. But I banished the thought—after all, my final minutes needn't be marred by rage.

Hotchkiss checked his watch and snapped it shut. "Five past," he said. "Let's get this over with. I won't be late for lunch."

McFarland gestured toward a well-worn patch of earth beneath the sprawling limbs of a massive oak. "There's the dance floor."

I gazed up at the Dueling Oak. It struck me that the tree and I had something in common: we'd both borne witness to countless pointless deaths.

"I'll wait by the horses," Charlotte said. She stepped close, cupped my face in her hands, and kissed me on the lips. Then she turned away.

That the worst morning of my life might also be, if not the best, then at least one touched by fleeting grace was not lost on me.

Jerome and Finn prepared the pistols while McFarland and I waited beneath the oak.

A yellow butterfly flitted past and settled on a branch above Charlotte, who stood with her eyes closed, lips moving in prayer or incantation. She clutched a gris-gris bag in one hand; in the other she rolled rosary beads between her fingers.

"I won't lie, Whitaker," McFarland said. "I was surprised by your choice. Pleased, but surprised."

"Why is that, J.W.?"

"Because honor doesn't come easy to the Northern man. He fights it tooth and nail, valuing his pretty little hide more than anything that truly matters. Ideals come second, if at all. But then it became clear to me: you're a man with a tenuous grip on life. You exist without a tribe. You stand in solitude." He lit a cigarette. "You might think of that negro boy over there, and that mulatto girl, as members of your tribe. But I assure you, they don't reciprocate the feeling."

Jerome and Finn approached with the pistols, and Jerome handed me mine. Its weight surprised me—it felt far heavier than the practice weapon from the day before. He gave my shoulder a squeeze. "Remember, Doc—hair trigger. Aim, breathe, tap."

I nodded.

"We'll call out seventeen paces, then give the command. When you hear it, turn, aim, breathe, squeeze. Got it? Nice and easy."

"Got it."

"Knock him dead, brother," Finn said, giving J.W. a light punch on the shoulder. "Lucky number seven."

"Let's get this over with!" Hotchkiss barked. "Antoine's stops serving lunch at one-thirty."

"You'll do fine," Jerome said.

I gripped the pistol tighter.

"Ready?" he said. "Turn."

McFarland and I turned our backs to each other. My stomach clenched, my breath caught, and the edges of my vision blurred. The clearing fell silent as the earth held its breath in anticipation of my death.

Charlotte stood beneath the branches. Her eyes were open now, her lips still moving. I thought I saw them form the words *I love you, Hiram T. Whitaker*, though it might also have been *Hallowed be Thy name, Thy kingdom come.*

"One." The word rang out in Jerome's voice, one I would miss terribly when I was gone, and in Finn's ugly, nasal drawl. I took the first step.

"Two," they called, their mismatched tones a jarring memory of a fiddle's double-stop at a long-ago dance. I saw my mother laughing as she spun around in her bright yellow dress. My sister's stumbling steps as she tried to mimic her. While Father stayed home to brood over some particularly challenging Commandment.

"Three." The number of letters I'd written to Father, stamped and sealed, then crushed and tossed away at the last moment, wasting three perfectly good stamps.

"Four." The number of us there'd been at my sixth birthday party, only days before Father reduced it to three.

"Five." The number of ingredients Charlotte said it took to make a proper Git-Me-a-Man potion. Too late now, I knew, to be the man she might have git.

"Six." The number of lashes I counted before I tried to help the man on the platform in Jackson Square. If I lived past this day, past "Seventeen," I would never forgive myself for having let it get past one.

"Seven." The number of letters I'd received from Father and thrown away unopened.

"Eight." The number of dead bodies I'd found in Saint Anne's.

"Nine." The number of feathers in White Wolf's headdress.

"Ten." The number of fingers with which Mother clutched my arm as she lay dying.

"Eleven." The number of children huddled in the tepees, arrayed in a gentle arc beneath snow-dusted trees, as the cavalry raiders rode through.

"Twelve." The number of disciples Jesus gave the power to heal every disease and affliction.

"Thirteen." The number of the Tarot card the fortune teller drew from the pack my first day in New Orleans. "Death. But don't worry, sweetie. The Death card doesn't always mean you're going to die. Sometimes it just means you have to let go of the past to be reborn. Depends on the next card." She flipped it. "Seven of Cups. Oh, yes—you're going to die."

"Fourteen." The number of candles on my birthday cake the day my sister died.

"Fifteen." The number of mounted cavalry from Fort Laramie who rode through Red Bear's camp, while the one in front, Lieutenant Grattan, screeched his threat to "Kill the lot of ya redskin animals!"

"Sixteen!" The number of times Mary Beth told me she loved me before she died. I counted every one of them and wrote them all down.

"Seventeen!" The—

"Fire!"

My heart exploded in my chest as though McFarland had shot me through the back before I could even turn. I froze, a statue in memory of myself. But then, feeling the heavy thump of my heart repeat—once, twice, thrice—I glanced down to see my vest and shirt unbloodied.

I turned and raised the heavy, malevolent thing to my eye.

The space beneath the oaks shifted, dimmed, then twisted inward toward the middle. At the center, the dark form of J.W. McFarland loomed, unwavering in the distance.

I aligned my sights on that form.

Steady, Hiram. Breathe.

I tapped the trigger.

The hammer fell with a sharp crack that rang out like a church bell inside my skull. A burst of smoke. A blinding flash. A jet of red flame. A second explosion jolted my arm.

The smoke cleared.

Silence.

McFarland stood unmoving in the distance, his shirt uncrimsoned. I dropped the pistol and patted my chest, my heart beating frantically.

Had we both missed?

He raised his hand. To wave at me, perhaps, as if to say, "Good show, old chap, honor restored, let us both carry on with our lives as if none of this ugliness had ever come to pass."

A shaft of sunlight pierced the treetops and glinted off the barrel of McFarland's raised pistol.

A distant *clank*. A cloud of smoke. A burst of flame.

White-hot pain tore through my chest. I gasped, the air stolen from my lungs, and stumbled. The rocky earth hurled toward me as the pain radiated outward and left me cold. Deafness and blindness descended upon me as I crashed into the ground.

Hands lie upon my body—Charlotte's, then Jerome's. They roll me over onto my back, unbutton my vest and shirt. Press a rag against my chest to sop up the blood pumping out. Shove a cotton plug into the hole. The pain begins to dull.

I'm cold.

My last chance to see Charlotte's face. I open my eyes.

It's not Charlotte's I see, but Jerome's, inches from mine, glistening with sweat. His lips move, but I can't make out the words.

Charlotte appears, just beyond him, eyes closed, lips moving. Her orange tignon sways, as if riding the cold breeze blowing through the oaks. Thick hands land on her shoulders like monstrous, grasping bugs and pull her away. Other hands descend on Jerome, clutching his neck, his forehead, his arms. He shouts—I feel his breath on my face—and struggles to break free. But they drag him away.

For a moment, the trees' dark canopy is all there is, and I believe I might rise through it into the sky beyond, away from this rocky, blood-soaked earth.

J.W. McFarland leans into view—grinning, a bead of sweat glistening at the tip of his nose. He looks away, down the length of his arm, past the rolled-up shirt cuff, to the pistol dangling from his white, claw-like fingers. He shifts it a few inches to the left and I stare into its lone black eye.

His lips move, and I read the words: "Mercy shot, Whicket. Nothing personal."

Goodbye, Charlotte.
His finger taps the trigger.

30

The smoke cleared to reveal a deep blue sky scattered with clouds. It was a familiar sky, a late fall Wyoming sky. There was a familiar sound too—that of a shovel's steel tip dragging through rocky earth, etching, most likely, a rectangle. It scraped so close to my ear that I felt the air shift against my skin.

"Yes sir, that should just about do it," said a low, rasping voice.

My head lolled to the side. A tall man in a black coat and top hat stood near my feet. He moved closer until I could see his face. One side was painted to resemble a skull, the hollow eye socket as real as any I'd seen in medical college. The other half was that of a man in his prime, the good eye glowing a radiant, crystalline blue.

"Sorry about your cat," I said. The words came out strange and flat in the quiet of the low hills. "We didn't mean to steal it. He just came along."

"Don't sweat it, Doc. He'll come home now. He's done what he set out to do."

I sat up and looked around.

Yes, I knew this place. The low, rolling hills. The distant pale mountains. The vast, empty sky. This barren wagon trail.

I stood up and brushed the dirt from my trousers. My shirt clung to me, soaked through. Not much time could have passed since McFarland shot me—I could still feel the blood bubbling from the hole in my chest, warming me against the chill of the prairie air.

Baron Sunday finished etching the rectangle around the place where I'd lay dying. He drove the shovel's tip into the earth with the heel of his boot and tossed aside a shovelful of rocky soil.

Beside the rectangle where he intended to bury me was another: the raised mound where I'd buried Mary Beth.

"No cross here, I see," he said. "Seems a little cold, don't it?"

"I'm not a Christian," I replied. "I don't believe in the cross."

"But she was, and she did. That's what matters here."

"Little good it did her. Little good it's done anyone."

"Trust in one's own beliefs is a wonderful thing, ain't it, Doc? Simplifies the struggles of a complex life, faith does." He drove the shovel deeper and tossed aside another shovelful. "You're bleeding pretty bad. At this rate, you'll have your humors balanced in no time. Ol' J.W.'ll have to send you a bill for medical services rendered."

I looked around, wondering where White Wolf and the other Indians were.

"Cavalry massacred the lot of 'em," he said, as if reading my mind. "Just a couple days ago. Or will do soon enough, I forget which. Something about a cow left behind, just over there, beyond that rise. Sick with anthrax, it was. One of the braves took it and butchered it back at camp. Boys from the fort claimed he stole it. Red Bear wouldn't give up the brave, so the Americans killed 'em all. Women and children too. Shame, really. Some of them little ones were the prettiest things you ever saw, with big green eyes that shined like a spring meadow after the rain."

I stared at Baron Sunday, shocked and heartbroken by the news. But I was equally shocked and heartbroken by the sudden gush of blood flowing from my chest. I stripped off my shirt and stuck a finger into the hole, trying to staunch the flow.

"Funny thing about all that blood you've been draining out of people, Doc."

"Funny? How so?"

"What do you reckon happens to all that air you breathe?"

I struggled to take a breath. What little air I could take in now bubbled straight out. "I never thought about it," I gasped.

"Anyone ever hold a pillow over your face till you were fit to pass out? An older brother, maybe, or a cousin? Ever had a friend get stuck under a log in the ol' swimming hole, but you couldn't pull 'em free till it was too late? Ever notice how people tend to die when they stop breathing?"

I didn't answer. I was too focused on the fiery agony of trying to breathe.

"Ain't no surprise, really," Sunday went on. "You might think your lungs are just hot air balloons, inflating and deflating for no particular reason but to lighten your step; or a bellows meant to stoke your inner fire. But that ain't the science of it. Breath is the life force. But how's it get from your lungs to the rest of you? To your organs and tissues and whatnot, where it can do some good? Tell me that."

"I don't know," I croaked. "I suppose some sort of balancing of pressures."

"Blood. That's how. When you bleed a man, you rob him of his life force. You send him on his way to the place he least wants to go."

"But I've healed hundreds of men through—"

"Leeching? Slicing open their veins with them medieval contraptions? You've killed far more than you've saved, Doc. You and your ilk."

"That's not true," I gurgled.

"No? Then you'll be the healthiest man alive soon enough."

The fresh grave was nearly a foot deep now. Sunday paused his digging and leaned on the shovel's handle.

"That's about how deep you put Mary Beth," he said. "Not a fair comparison, of course. Seeing as how you dug her grave with your bare hands. Bled a fair bit then too, didn't you? Your fingertips all scraped to the bone. Must have felt invigorating, made you feel like a man. But here, why don't you lie down in that hole, stretch yourself out and check the fit? The earth's nice and cool. Time we got you out of this execrable heat."

I got down on my hands and knees, crawled into the hole, stretched out, and lay back. The earth was cool, he was right about that.

"Perfect fit," he said. "Just as I knew it would be. Now, you lie there until all that bleeding heals you right up." He winked. And as he did, the human side of his face began to change, flesh giving way to bone. The one blue eye faded from radiant sapphire to pale, milky periwinkle.

Napoleon appeared at the edge of the grave. He looked down at me, whiskers twitching, then leapt in and rubbed himself against the soles of my feet.

"Get out of there, cat, while I cover him up," Sunday said. "Unless you want to spend eternity here in Wyoming with Doc Whitaker."

He surveyed the surroundings—the rolling hills, the plains that stretched to the edges of the earth, the wide blue sky. "Not the worst of fates, I'll grant you that." Two hawks circled overhead. "Though if I were you, I'd keep an eye on them buzzards."

Napoleon climbed onto my chest and settled beside the wound, from which blood still seeped.

"Go away, Napoleon," I whispered, my voice hoarse and fading. "This is no place for you. Go home."

I closed my eyes and listened to the cold breeze whistle through the grave. I smelled frankincense, and thought it must grow in these parts. And chamomile, sandalwood, and sage.

"Papa Legba, open the gate and let the spirits enter. Saint Michael, protect us with your sword. Saint Expedite, hurry to help us."

Where were these words coming from? The voice was low, warm, female.

Charlotte's.

I tried to move, but a jolt of pain shot through me.

Someone laid a cold compress across my forehead.

"Heavenly Father," Charlotte's voice continued, "I come before you with a humble heart. The Lord sustains him on his sickbed; in his illness, you restore him to full health."

Fingertips pressed against my wrist.

"His pulse is fading. Should I get Marie?" Jerome's voice now.

"Almighty God, I beg you—"

"*Merde*. I don't feel anything. He's not breathing."

"Heal him, Lord, and I will be healed; save him, and I will be saved. Benevolent spirits, protective saints, loas—I beg you, don't abandon him."

"This wasn't supposed to happen," Jerome said. "He wasn't supposed to die."

<h1 style="text-align:center">31</h1>

I opened my eyes to a circle of flickering candle flames. Frankincense smoke drifted in the air.

"Oh, my God," Jerome said.

"Praise Jesus," said Charlotte.

"The Lord sustains him," came a voice from the foot of the bed.

I lifted my head to see Marie Laveau standing there, a silver cross raised in one hand, a gris-gris bag held high in the other.

For a moment, I didn't know whether I was alive, dead, or somewhere in between. I looked at them in turn: Charlotte, smiling radiantly, one hand pressed to her chest; Jerome, lips parted, eyes shining, as if on the verge of tears; and Marie, calm and still, as if she'd long since foreseen this moment.

Somehow, I was alive.

Something rested atop the dressings piled on my chest. I felt for it and found a crucifix strung to a rosary. There was something else, too, something wet and meaty. Panicking, believing it was a piece of my chest sticking through the bandages, I yanked my hand away.

"What is that?" I sputtered.

Charlotte placed a hand on my shoulder.

"It's a beef heart, darling Hiram."

Was it, I wondered, the same beef heart she'd bought from the butcher all those weeks ago? Had she known even then this day would come?

Casting these thoughts aside, I touched my face, then my forehead, searching for a bullet hole; all I found were scabs.

"I don't understand," I said. "McFarland shot me in the face. How...?"

"The pistol blew up in his hand," Jerome said.

I propped myself up on my elbows. The beef heart and rosary slid down toward my belly. "Is he...?"

"The explosion blew his hand off. He might've survived, but the ball went through his eye and into his brain."

"He's dead," Charlotte said. "You should have seen him —walking around in circles with one hand and one eyeball, hollering, 'What happened? Did I get him?' It was *très amusant*."

"Doctor Pembroke tried to save him," Jerome said. "But he died before they got him to the hospital."

I sank back into the pillow and stared at the ceiling. Despite everything, I felt pity for J.W. McFarland—the violent absurdity of his life, the pathetic, farcical nature of his death. He, like all men, must have been born a decent human being.

Mustn't he have?

"I'll be going now," Marie Laveau said. "Mrs. Beasley's expecting me to do her hair at four."

* * *

I convalesced for several days more, sleeping most of the time. Jerome and Charlotte took turns nursing me back to health. I drank three cups of Charlotte's Live-Long Tea every day. I read the newspaper. There was no new mention of the fetus-robbing fiend of the cathedral gardens, and Jerome said he hadn't heard anything more about it. The *Picayune* carried a brief note by the editor reporting that one J.W. McFarland, director of the Medical Board and Board of Health, had died following a firearms accident—and that it was hoped that this might speed the allocation of municipal health funds.

I ate whatever they gave me without asking about the strange flavors and textures. Candles and incense burned night and day. Smoke drifted through the room like Wyoming clouds.

On the fourth or fifth day, I sat propped against a pile of pillows while Jerome changed the dressings on my chest wound.

"How did McFarland's pistol happen to blow up?" I asked. I'd been mulling over this question for some time.

"Finn," Jerome said.

I stared at him while he repacked the wound with herbal paste. "Finn made J.W.'s gun blow up in his hand?"

"That's right," he said, pressing a fresh pad into place and taping it down. "Plugged the barrel with lead instead of cotton before the mercy shot."

I tried to make sense of it but couldn't. "Why would he do that?"

"For Arabella."

I wondered if the explosion had rattled something loose in my brain; I couldn't for the life of me figure out why Finn McFarland would do such a thing. "I don't—"

"They've been in love for some time, Doctor Whitaker. Finn McFarland is the father of Arabella's son. And now he's the sole owner of the McFarland estate."

At last, I understood.

"Call me Hiram, Jerome."

"Hiram."

"So Finn freed her," I said.

"He can't free her. But she's safe, for now."

A few days later, a letter arrived from Bridget O'Malley, my father's caretaker. It was brief and to the point:

> Your father has only a few weeks left to live.
> His final wish is to see you one last time.

Later that same day, a message came from Sister Genevieve of The Daughters of Charity:

> I write to inform you that Archbishop Antoine Blanc plans to reopen Saint Anne's Hospital. We are in need of a good doctor and pray you are able to return to your post.

32

After a grueling steamboat journey up the Mississippi and Ohio Rivers, followed by an interminable train ride through a countryside of leafless orchards, frozen fields, and snowbound villages, I stood on the porch of a modest home in a quiet Philadelphia neighborhood. A biting wind cut through my coat.

My hand hovered near the door, then dropped. I turned to the snow-dusted street, then back. I knocked softly. After a moment, the door opened. A middle-aged man in a gray wool coat squinted at me, as if struggling to place me.

"It's me, Mr. Johansson. Hiram."

Mary Beth's father rocked back slightly, as if seeing a ghost. "Bernadette," he called over his shoulder. "It's Hiram at the door."

Mary Beth's mother appeared beside him, wearing a white knit shawl over a black dress. Her dark hair, pinned into a simple bun, was now streaked with white. Despite seeming to have aged a decade in the year and a half since I'd seen her, she still strongly resembled Mary Beth.

They stared at me in silence, long enough that I thought they might send me away. My body growing numb, I tapped my feet, trying to warm them.

"Invite him in, Gerry," Mrs. Johansson said at last.

"Would you like to come in, Hiram?"

"Yes, sir, thank you."

They stepped aside, and I entered Mary Beth's childhood home, a place I thought I'd never set foot in again. Despite the grief that must have lingered here, everything felt warm and inviting: the simple furniture, the fire glowing in the hearth, the mantel lined with framed drawings of Mary Beth. Even the cross and framed Bible verses on the wall added to the welcoming warmth.

"Have a seat," Mrs. Johansson said. "I'll put on some tea."

I sat on the sofa, and Mr. Johansson settled into a rocking chair, rocking once, with a quiet squeak.

"So, what brings you to Philadelphia?" he asked.

"My father's dying," I said. "I'm on my way to visit him in New York. But I came here hoping I might tell you what happened to your daughter."

The fire crackled. Wind buffeted the walls.

"We received your letter from New Orleans," he said.

Mrs. Johansson returned with the tea and offered me a cup.

"Thank you," I said, grateful for the distraction—and the warmth of the cup in my hands.

She took the chair beside her husband.

"Said she fell ill with the cholera, up in Wyoming," Mr. Johansson said. "And died there."

"Yes, sir, that's right."

"I guess I don't really understand what brings you here. Unless it's to offer your condolences in person, which isn't necessary. It won't change anything. It won't bring her back."

"I came to tell you some things I failed to include in my letter. What really happened."

They stared at me. I wanted to look away, but didn't. I was tired of looking away.

"What do you mean?" Mrs. Johansson said.

I took a deep breath.

I recounted the journey briefly—the delays, the flooded tracks, the broken boiler, the struck cows, missing the wagon train at Independence. The Johanssons knew most of this from my letter. Now I touched upon only the essentials: using half our funds to buy a wagon and two horses, struggling for provisions, breaking an axle, falling weeks behind the wagon train despite our best efforts to catch up.

"Then," I said, "as we rested along the North Platte River, twenty miles east of the fort, Mary Beth fell ill."

The Johanssons watched me intently. I had decided I would tell them as much as I could without upsetting them needlessly.

"She had gone down to the river while I stayed behind to watch camp. After a while, night began to fall, and I went to find her. I found her kneeling on the shore, trembling. Her face was pale, glistening with sweat. She'd suffered from diarrhea and vomiting. She whispered that she couldn't move her legs. I knew right away: it was cholera.

"I took off my shirt, soaked it in the river, and bathed her to cool her down. I carried her back to the wagon and tried to make her drink what little water we had, but she spat it up. I gave her laudanum to ease her pain, then decided to start bleeding her, before it was too late."

I paused to gauge their reactions, not wishing to upset them with the details of their daughter's last hours.

"I found the scarifier in my medical satchel—a small instrument with several blades, meant to draw blood quickly. I started with Mary Beth's right wrist. It soon ran dry, so I switched to the left. It was then that my first symptoms hit."

I recalled how the first cramp had struck me like a mule's kick to the gut. I dropped the scarifier, stumbled from the wagon, fell to my knees, shat my pants, and vomited.

Mary Beth! I cried. There was no answer.

A frigid wind blew through the camp. It started to rain. Desperate with thirst, I rolled onto my back and tried to catch raindrops on my tongue. I prayed for the sky to open, but it was only a brief sprinkle.

After several dry heaves, my stomach calmed. I managed to pull off my soiled trousers.

The Johanssons were watching me. How long had I been lost in memory?

"After a brief spell of stomach discomfort," I continued, "I stood and went to the wagon. 'Mary Beth?' I asked. 'Are you all right?'

"She was barely breathing. I tried to coax the last few drops of water from the canteen into her mouth. She spat those up, too."

Mary Beth, please don't die, I begged her. *You're all I have left.*

"I considered packing up camp and setting out toward Fort Laramie for help. But it was two days' away, and I knew I couldn't make it."

I paused. I'd been ready to give up, to lie down beside her and hope we'd both recover—or die together—when another cramp shot through my bowels. I scrambled out of the wagon and stumbled into the bushes, where I squatted in agony.

"Just then, I heard horses. It might have been trappers who could help us, but it might also have been Indians. And this close to Fort Laramie, we were deep in their territory.

"Three Indians on horseback appeared at the edge of our camp. Two carried bows, the third a rifle. One dismounted and walked toward the wagon. Another rode closer to me, stopping just a few yards away. The one on foot continued toward the wagon.

"Afraid of what he might do to Mary Beth, I stood up. 'Stop!' I yelled.

"But he didn't stop. He looked inside the wagon. I staggered out of the bushes but one of the others raised his rifle and shook his head."

I raised my hands in surrender. *Please, just let me put my trousers on.*

"You must have been terrified," Mrs. Johansson said.

"I was."

"Did those savages harm our girl?" Mr. Johansson said.

I held my tongue at the word "savages" and only shook my head.

The Indians exchanged words. I grabbed my other pair of pants and pulled them on.

"'Don't touch her,' I said. 'She's sick. She needs to be bled.' But one of them climbed into the wagon. I lunged toward him, but one of the others grabbed me into a wrestling hold. The one in the wagon climbed out and retrieved a canteen from his horse. 'Wife, water,' he said.

"The one holding me let go. 'Careful.'

"I climbed into the wagon, where the brave was dribbling water onto Mary Beth's lips. He handed me the canteen. 'Drink.'

"I took it and swallowed a mouthful.

"They didn't seem to want to harm us. They built a fire and prepared tea. The tallest one sat cross-legged and began chanting some sort of prayer.

"I turned to Mary Beth to resume bleeding her. As I applied the scarifier, the chanting brave stood, lit a bundle of herbs, and approached. When he saw what I was doing, horror crossed his face. He grabbed my arm.

"'What are you doing?' I yelled. 'Get away! Let me go!'

"'No hurt wife,' he said.

"'Hurt her? I'm trying to save her!'

"He let go but didn't back away. He waved the herbs in the air and blew smoke into the wagon. Another appeared with a cup of tea. 'Wife. Drink. Medicine.'

"I didn't take it. I ignored their help and turned back to bleeding Mary Beth."

I stopped. The Johanssons stared at me.

I took a breath and steeled myself to say the thing I had needed to say for some time. "I can't be certain whether your daughter might have lived if it weren't for me. But I believe she would have. I think they could have saved her—if I'd let them."

Mr. Johansson sat stone-faced. Tears streamed down Mrs. Johansson's cheeks.

"If you'd like me to stop—"

"No. Just go on," Mr. Johansson said, handing his wife a handkerchief.

"I continued bleeding her, measuring her pulse and breath. But instead of growing stronger, they faded. 'Mary Beth,' I whispered. 'You have to get stronger. You have to live.' I kissed her hand. It was already cold. 'Please don't go,' I said. 'I love you.'

"I collapsed.

"When I came to, I was on a bed of furs in a tepee. Sage and sweet grass smoke hung in the air. An old Indian man sat in the corner holding an eagle feather in his hand. A young woman in a deerskin dress sat next to him. They were the tribe's medicine man and his daughter. This was their healing tepee.

"I had no idea where I was, or how long I'd been asleep. 'Where's my wife?' I asked. But they didn't understand.

"The woman left and returned with a brave I recognized. He sat beside the medicine man, nodded at me, and smiled—as if happy to see I was recovering.

"'My wife,' I asked, 'where is she?' His smile faded."

Mr. Johansson sat rigid, gripping the rocking chair's armrests. Mrs. Johansson held her hand to her chest.

"I knew what that meant. I would never see her again, never hear her laugh. Never see her smile. Everything we'd dreamed of—a life of adventure, a life together in California—had vanished.

"I knew I had failed her. She was smart, kind, funny. She didn't deserve what happened to her. I would have given everything to trade places with her.

'Where is she?' I asked. 'Take me to her.'

"Two braves—White Wolf and Cold Moon—lifted me between them and carried me through the camp, a dozen tepees standing in a half-circle open to the west. Cooking smoke drifted in the air. They carried me through the trees that bordered the camp. When we emerged, I saw it on a low hill: a platform of woven sticks set atop cottonwood poles. A blanket-wrapped bundle lay on top."

Mrs. Johansson may have made a sound then, but it might only have been the distant cry of a hawk circling somewhere overhead.

"They brought me closer, then set me down and sat beside me."

There in the Johanssons' parlor, I could smell the cooking smoke again, drifting through the tall grass.

"I wept before Mary Beth's funeral scaffold. When there was nothing left, White Wolf and Cold Moon helped me to my feet.

"'Take her down,' I told them. 'She'd want to be buried in the earth.'

"They didn't understand, so I gestured bringing her down and mimed digging a hole and laying her in it. White Wolf crouched and mimicked a wolf digging and tearing at something with its jaws. But I insisted.

"They brought her down and laid her on the grass. She was wrapped in blankets, one corner draped over her face. Even then, I refused to believe she was gone. I held on to the hope that when I pulled back the corner, it would be someone else. Or it would be Mary Beth, but she'd awaken and smile, refreshed from her long nap.

"I folded back the corner. Of course it was her."

But not the Mary Beth I remembered. Time had taken her from me.

"'How long have I been in your camp?' I asked. White Wolf didn't understand, so I traced the sun's arc with my hand, and held up my fingers. One, two, three? He nodded and spread five fingers. Five days.

"I got down on my hands and knees and, with Baron Sunday standing only a few inches away, I began to dig."

"What did you just say?" Mr. Johansson asked.

"I said I began to dig."

"You said something about a Baron Sunday."

"Did I?"

"Who is that?"

"He... It's difficult to explain."

"A baron was there while you dug our daughter's grave?" Mrs. Johansson said.

"Yes, ma'am. But he wasn't a real baron. He was just... a spirit."

"A spirit?" Mr. Johansson said.

"Yes, sir."

"But why was he there?" Mrs. Johansson asked.

I had often asked myself the same thing. Now, I believed I knew the answer.

"To take me to New Orleans."

They exchanged a look.

"But why did he want to take you there?" Mrs. Johansson asked.

"I'm not certain," I said. "But I believe it was to help kill a man and free his slave."

Mr. Johansson glanced at his wife, then back at me. "So, you buried her. With that baron spirit there."

"Yes, sir."

"Did you mark her grave?"

"I did."

"With a cross?"

"With rocks."

"In the shape of a cross?"

I shook my head.

He took a sip of tea, his hands trembling. "What did you say, aloud, as you stood over her grave?"

"I begged her to forgive me. I told her I loved her. That I'd love her until the day I died."

"Did she receive a Christian burial? I understand there weren't many ministers out there in the Wyoming wilderness, but did you at least say a few words from the Bible?"

"No, sir. I didn't."

He lowered his head. Mrs. Johansson began to weep again.

I stood. "I should be going. I'm sorry to have troubled you."

They stood too.

"I know you can't forgive me," I said. "I wouldn't ask it of you. But if it's any comfort, I haven't forgiven myself, and I don't think I ever will."

"That's not true, Hiram," Mr. Johansson said.

Mrs. Johansson stepped forward and hugged me, resting her head against my chest. "Of course we forgive you. And you must find a way to forgive yourself."

"We're Christians," Mr. Johansson said. "You did what you thought was right. You tried to save her. You just went about it the wrong way."

Mrs. Johansson stepped back, her hands resting on my arms. "But you must give her a Christian burial. And a proper marker for her grave."

33

Even after a month-long journey, during which I'd had endless hours to imagine what it would be like to see my father again, I wasn't prepared for it when I stepped off the train at the Hudson Railroad Depot in lower Manhattan. I didn't even know whether he was alive or dead. All I knew was that I should go straight to him during what must be his final days.

Instead, I checked into a hotel in Five Points, just a few blocks from my childhood home. After cleaning up, I stepped outside into the chilly evening air. Snowflakes landed on my sleeves, and at first I mistook them for ash.

I wandered the streets aimlessly before settling in a café, where I ordered coffee and an apple tart. I leafed through a discarded newspaper. When my cup was empty and only crumbs remained on my plate, I took a notebook from my coat pocket, in which I'd written two addresses: one for Patience Dufilho, the other for Emma Smith.

Emma was staying just a few minutes' walk from where I sat.

* * *

My heart pounded as I climbed the stairwell to the third floor of 54 Bleecker Street. At each landing, I paused to reconsider. But I had to see her. I had to know.

I knocked.

Footsteps. A click from the chain lock. The door opened an inch or two, and Emma peered out.

"Yes?" she said, failing to recognize me.

While I must have changed completely, she looked exactly the same: young, fresh, pink-cheeked, sparkle-eyed. She'd escaped New Orleans before the plague could steal her vitality and youth.

Just seeing her like this filled me with warmth.

"It's me," I said. "Hiram."

Her eyes widened. "Hiram!"

The door flew open. She leapt into my arms and kissed me on the cheek. "Hiram, Hiram, Hiram," she said. "You're alive! You're here! Oh my God."

I eased her down.

She cupped my face in her hands. "From the newspapers, I thought everyone in New Orleans was dead."

She took me by the hand and led me inside. The parlor glowed with golden firelight.

We talked late into the night. She told me about her life in New York and the hospital where she worked, treating minor injuries like sprained ankles and cut fingers. No one had died during her time there—neither patient nor staff. She recounted her last day in New Orleans: finding everyone dead at Saint Anne's, her ensuing panic, her escape. She apologized again for not saying goodbye.

I might have done the same thing and fled from that cursed place had I known she'd already left the city. But I kept that to myself.

I told her about my father's illness and how I had come to New York to see him and, if possible, to settle affairs with Patience and Sarah Dufilho.

"And then?" she asked. "You'll stay in New York, won't you? It's so much better here. So much healthier. So much less... cruel. And there are jobs here for someone like you. There are even openings at New York Hospital. Wouldn't that be wonderful, for us to work together again?"

I took her hand. "I wasn't a good person, Emma. I've needed to tell you that for a long time. I was terrible."

"What are you talking about? You're one of the kindest, least terrible people I've ever known."

I shook my head. "You were right about everything." I let go of her hand. "I was insufferable."

"That's all in the past," she said. "You're here in New York now, and you must stay here. And while you look for a job, you can stay with me—if you'd like. You know, if you'd rather not stay at your father's house."

"Here?"

"Yes! I have an extra room. Wouldn't it be perfect?"

"I'll think about it."

"Promise me you will."

I woke to faded, chipped pink paint. I was naked and tangled in sweat-soaked sheets. My head pounded.

I remembered Emma opening a bottle of wine. But after that, nothing. I rolled onto my back, the sheets bunching in a knot against my spine. I considered the possibility that Emma was in the bed beside me. I turned my head.

She wasn't there.

I sat up and looked around, but there was little to see: an empty bedside table, a plain dresser. No art on the walls. This wasn't Emma's room, then. It was the extra room she'd mentioned.

I sighed with relief.

I got out of bed, crossed to the window, and pulled the curtains open. Pale, cold light spilled into the room. Outside, a delivery wagon trundled past, but the street was otherwise deserted. It must have been barely past dawn.

I dressed and walked quietly through the apartment. In the parlor, four empty wine bottles stood on the table like giant chess pieces. Emma's bedroom door was ajar. I hesitated, then peeked in. She was asleep in her frilly white pajamas, snoring softly.

I shouldn't just sneak away, I thought. But if she'd drunk as much as I had, it was best to let her sleep.

I snuck away.

Patience Dufilho lived in a three-story brownstone in Gramercy Park, with a small, manicured garden behind a wrought iron fence. I let myself in through the gate and climbed the steps to the front door. As I reached for the brass knocker, I paused, taking in the quiet grandeur of the place. It was the home of someone with means, whether by marriage or family fortune. While so much still hung in the balance for Jerome, Charlotte, Sarah Dufilho, and her children, the fate of the Dufilho townhouse in New Orleans struck me as almost inconsequential to Patience. Her continued efforts on their behalf, then, made plain the depth of her good-heartedness.

I reflected on all that had happened since I first met her in Jackson Square, where I'd gone to watch a whipping in the rain. I lifted the knocker and rapped it against the door. Moments later, it opened to reveal a stout, middle-aged maid in a long white apron and frilled cap.

"Yes?" she said.

"Good afternoon, miss. My name is Hiram Whitaker. I'm an old friend of Madam Dufilho's. I'm here to pay her a visit."

"Old friend?"

"Yes."

"You wish to see her regarding—?"

"A social visit, mostly. But it concerns a house, in New Orleans."

"I see. One moment."

She closed the door. A few minutes later, she returned and ushered me into the front parlor.

"Madam has been resting. She's been quite busy lately, you know. But she's eager to see you. Can I get you something? Tea? Brandy?"

"Brandy would be fine."

As I waited, I took in the room: high ceilings adorned with intricate moldings, polished hardwood floors that gleamed in the soft light, heavy velvet curtains framing tall windows, and furniture so elegant it seemed to belong to another world.

My thoughts drifted. I remembered my first night in the master bedroom of the Dufilho townhouse, after ten long months in that dingy, foul-smelling room above the cigar factory. Life had been harsh in that little room, but it had been simple, too. When it rained, filthy black water leaked through the ceiling and soaked my bed. Bedbugs bit me while I slept. Rats rummaged through my meager food stores, their scratching and squealing waking me from dreams that were the sweetest part of my life.

Yet those things, at least, had been certain, predictable. Perhaps that was what I needed: certainty and predictability. A stable, ordinary life. A bank job, perhaps, or—

"Hiram!"

Patience and I caught up over tea and sandwiches, then retired to the library with glasses of brandy. Though modest in size, the library struck me as wonderfully luxurious. Two walls were lined with shelves packed with books, while a third displayed mementos from New Orleans. How lovely it would be, I thought, to convert the third-floor medicine storage room on Chartres Street into a library like this.

"Have you read all of these?" I asked, running my fingers along the spines.

"Not all, not yet," she said. "The Austens, of course. The Coopers, the Dickenses. I've just finished *Uncle Tom's Cabin*. Sensational. If that book doesn't put an end to slavery, then nothing will. Ah! Here we go."

She pulled a thickly stuffed folder from the shelf and handed it to me.

I sat on the brown leather couch and opened the folder. Inside were letters, court filings, and correspondence between Patience, Sarah, and their lawyers.

"The one on top," Patience said, "is the most interesting. And the most unfortunate."

It was a letter from Sarah's attorney, summarizing the dispute over Louis Dufilho's will and estate. According to him, the notary who had supposedly witnessed the addendum to Louis Dufilho's will—granting Stella France or her heir, Charlotte, a one-quarter share of the Chartres Street house—now swore under oath that he had never seen such a document. Charlotte's own lawyer, J.T. Farmer, Esquire, also denied any knowledge of it.

They claimed it was a forgery. Charlotte's forgery.

Sarah Dufilho's attorneys had issued an ultimatum: if Charlotte relinquished her claim to the house, they would let the matter rest. If she refused, they would proceed with criminal charges for fraud. Once the matter was resolved, the townhouse would be sold.

I tried to reread the letter, but the words refused to come into focus. I looked up at Patience, who stood by the window, gazing out at a small pear tree in the garden.

"This can't be true, can it?" I said.

"I don't think so. I never knew Charlotte well, but that will reads precisely like something my late husband would have written." She turned to face me. "I know for a fact he kept a *placée* while he was married to Sarah. He told me so himself."

"Do you think Charlotte's lawyer and the notary were bribed? By Sarah's people?"

"That's what must have happened, I'm afraid."

I looked down at the letter again. "What can I do? Should I report the bribes to the authorities?"

"I don't think there's anything you *can* do, Hiram. Sometimes life simply conspires against one, and we must carry on in spite of it."

34

The next morning, I ate a breakfast of tea and porridge at the hotel, then set off for New York University in Greenwich Village. There, the snow-dusted pathways felt eerily unchanged, and my steps led me to my old student boarding house on the east side of campus. Looking up at the third floor, I saw that the only open window belonged to my former room.

Just as I was about to continue on my way, a young man appeared at the window. Clean-shaven, with dark, wavy hair, he looked vaguely familiar. I watched him for a long moment as he gazed out at the gray skyline before I recognized him. As I waited to see if he might look down and notice the older, less naïve version of himself, another figure appeared beside him. Tall and slender, dressed in a black suit, he wore a top hat so high it nearly grazed the ceiling. The left side of his face was painted to resemble a human skull.

Noticing me below, Baron Sunday tipped his hat.

I nodded, then turned away and walked toward my childhood home on MacDougal Street, which I reached within minutes.

Had it always been so close? For two years, I'd lived only a short walk from my father's house and never once visited. Six years had passed in total since I'd seen him. Six Thanksgivings, six Christmases spent alone or with others like me who claimed "no living relatives." How had my father passed those days? Perhaps his brother's family had come down from Rochester, or he'd visited my mother's family in Boston. Perhaps he'd spent them alone.

I stood on the sidewalk, taking in the house. The paint was faded and peeling. Brambles choked the garden. Weeds spilled over the walkway.

I followed the path, climbed the steps, and knocked on the front door, nervous about what lay on the other side.

No answer.

I knocked again.

It's too late, I thought. I could never undo any of it.

I turned and descended the steps, pausing halfway to remember Heather and me playing jacks and tiddly-winks right here, on these steps.

Halfway to the street, I heard the door creak open behind me.

"Hello?"

I turned. "Bridget?"

Bridget O'Malley stood in the doorway, wearing a faded black calico dress, frayed wool shawl, scuffed leather boots. Her hair, once strawberry blond, had turned white. She'd come to work as a maid after Mother died, then stayed on as my father's caretaker. She'd been in her thirties then, but now must be in her fifties.

"You've come home," she said.

"Am I too late?"

"Your da's still alive, if that's what you're askin'."

Was it?

I didn't move.

"Why don't you come in and see him before it *is* too late."

I climbed the steps. Bridget led me into the parlor.

The first thing I noticed was the wallpaper. Once vibrant with bright green vines curling around pink and red roses, the colors were muted now, veiled in gray.

Bridget left and returned with a tray of tea which she set on the table where Heather and I had once held séances with the other neighborhood children.

"Shall I close the window?" she asked. "I know it's cold, but your father likes it that way. The sickness makes him hot."

"No, thank you."

It didn't feel cold to me at all.

"He's lived far longer than anyone expected, you know. But now he's wasted away to skin and bone. His chest rattles and he coughs up blood when he's asleep—which, mercifully, is most of the time. It's for the best, though. When he's awake, he suffers something awful."

"Does he take anything for the pain? Opium, laudanum?"

"He refuses such things. Always has."

"Do you know why?"

"You would ask, being a proper doctor and all."

I nodded.

"If God wants your father to suffer," she said, "then I can't fathom why. He don't deserve it. But your da's always made a point of following God's plan. I s'pose you already know that."

"Then you know what happened," I said.

"He told me. Says it's why he hasn't seen you since you went away. Why you don't answer his letters."

"Did he ever express any regrets?"

"Course not. He followed God's plan. There's nought to regret in that."

"But what if God's plan is wrong?"

She narrowed her eyes, drew a rosary from her apron, and rolled the beads between her fingers.

"The meaning of right and wrong comes from God," she said. "Might as well ask me what if ducks barked and dogs quacked."

I slipped my hand into my pocket and touched the *Simbi veve* amulet Charlotte had given me before I stepped onto the boat in New Orleans.

The loa Simbi will heal you and protect you, she had said.

"I suppose you're right."

"Course I am."

We drank our tea. The repetitive, mechanical sound of the grandfather clock's pendulum grew louder, echoing through the room.

"Would you like to visit your father now? He'll be sleeping, but I can wake him if you like."

"Would you mind if I looked around first? It's been a while since I've seen the house."

"Not at all. Take your time. You know your way around."

I stood. "Thank you for the tea."

"Course."

I went upstairs to my old bedroom, the first room on the left. It was mostly as I'd left it. The same novels on the shelf. A sketchbook and fountain pen resting on the desk. Cobwebs in the corners. The faint smell of mildew.

I pushed open the window to let in some fresh air, then sat on the bed. The springs creaked under my weight.

I opened the sketchbook and flipped through the pages. Drawings of Heather, mostly, her face captured from different angles. Some doodles of odd geometric shapes—swirling lines, crosses, star-like figures. I'd always enjoyed drawing things like that.

As I was about to turn the page, one of the sketches stopped my hand.

I pulled the *Simbi veve* amulet from my pocket and held it beside the drawing. The intricate, symmetrical designs were nearly identical.

Somehow, I wasn't surprised.

I closed the sketchbook and stood. The mattress groaned softly, as if reluctant to let me go after all these years.

I walked down the hall, past Heather's room, to the sickroom at the end. The door seemed stuck at first, or locked from within. But with a firm twist of the knob and a hard push, it gave way. I stepped inside, leaving the door slightly ajar behind me.

The curtains were drawn, the only light coming from a candle flickering on the bedside table. A bouquet of roses drooped in a vase beside it, their brown petals scattered across the table.

Mother lay gaunt and pale in the bed, her hair tangled and damp with sweat. Her cheeks were sunken, her lips cracked, her breath shallow and labored. A patchwork quilt was bunched around her legs. A small locket rested on her chest. Beneath the smell of sickness, a faint trace of lavender, her favorite perfume, lingered.

Kneeling beside the bed, gripping Mother's left hand, was Father. In his other hand, a Bible.

"Heavenly Father, I kneel before you with a humble heart." His voice was calm, almost as if he were speaking to an old friend. He flipped to a frayed blue bookmark and ran his finger down the page. "Yes, here: Lord, heal this woman as You have healed the sick. By Your words, we are healed."

Mother turned her head slightly. The ghost of a smile passed over her face. I'd forgotten that smile, Mother's beautiful smile. I'd only remembered her look of suffering.

Father dipped a rag into a bowl of water, wrung it out, and laid it across her forehead.

"The Lord sustains her on her sickbed," he read. "Restore her to full health."

Mother's eyes fell closed.

"Please," Father whispered.

For a while, the room was silent, but for the sound of three souls breathing. Soon the quiet was shattered by Mother's violent coughing. When it passed, she turned her head and spat green phlegm into a rag. Father took it and gently wiped her lips clean.

"Should I get Doctor Johnson?" I asked.

Father's head jerked as if he'd forgotten I was there, as if an uninvited stranger had violated his private, intimate moment with his wife and his God. He glanced over his shoulder.

"She'll be well soon enough," he said. "God will see to it."

He turned back to the Bible. His hand trembled as he turned to another page.

"Heal her, Lord, and I will be healed. Save her, and I will be saved."

Mother sank deeper into the bed.

Father set the Bible aside and pressed his hands together in prayer. Beads of sweat glistened on his forehead.

"I'm begging you, God. Heal my beloved wife. She's done nothing wrong. She doesn't deserve this."

"Doctor Johnson will know what to do," I said, trying to keep my voice steady despite my rising panic.

Father turned and fixed me with a hard stare. "Remain silent or get out. Don't dare tell me a man can do what God cannot."

He turned back to Mother and gripped her hand.

"Restore her health and heal her wounds, sayeth the Lord. Jeremiah, 30:17."

Mother let out a dry, painful gasp that rocked Father back on his knees.

I clutched the amulet in my pocket. Charlotte's words echoed in my head: *Guaranteed to heal and protect.* I remembered how she'd placed it in my palm and closed my fingers around it. *Use it when you need it. Promise me you will.*

Desperate to save Mother, I stepped forward to place the amulet on her chest.

Father's arm shot out to block me. "Back, boy," he hissed.

"She's not breathing," I said. "Someone's got to help her."

"Almighty God!" Father cried, clutching Mother's hand, eyes turning to the ceiling. "I beg of you—please, save her."

It was in that moment that I understood how deeply, and for how long, my father had suffered. And I, just as deeply, wished there were some way I could take away his pain.

But it was too late.

Father stood up. "Get out," he said.

I left the room. And as I did, I looked back to see a man climb into a bed and lie beside his dead wife. I closed the door, pressed my ear against it, and listened to my father's broken weeping.

"God. Dolores. God. Dolores. God. Dolores."

I went to the other door and placed my ear against it. Hearing nothing, I opened it.

Heather lay in the bed, a small, fragile figure swaddled in blankets, golden curls spilling across the pillow. Her gaunt face was pale as porcelain, with a feverish flush upon her cheeks. A mist seemed to drift across her pale blue eyes as she glanced in my direction but failed to recognize me. Her tiny hands clutched Anna, her beloved rag doll, to her chest.

Father knelt at her bedside, head bowed in prayer. A candle on the dresser cast flickering light over his Bible.

"Thank you, God, for Your blessings," he said. "My beautiful wife, who now rests in glory on Your knee. My daughter, Heather." He lifted his head. "The Lord is my shepherd; I shall not want. He maketh me to lie down in green pastures: He leadeth me beside the still waters. He restoreth my soul."

He took Heather's hand and squeezed it gently. "You're going to be all right, little one. He will heal you." He held a glass of water to her lips. "You have to take it," he said, his voice trembling.

She didn't respond.

He set down the glass, dipped a rag into a bowl of water, wrung it out, and touched it to her lips before setting it aside.

"God," he said, "Heather, my little girl here, is sick with the cholera. I don't know why You gave it to her, just as I don't know why You gave it to her mother. She's a child, and she's done nothing wrong. I know Your plans are perfect, even when I don't understand them. But, please, Lord, spare her."

He sat back and closed his eyes. "Lay your healing hands upon her fevered head," he said. Then, more urgently: "Ask, and it will be given to you. Matthew, 7:7. God, I'm asking. The prayer of faith will save the sick. James, 5:15. My baby is sick; I, your faithful servant, am praying. I don't ask for much. I never have. But I'm asking you now for this one small thing."

"I should get Doctor Johnson," I said.

Startled by my presence, Father glanced at me but said nothing. He turned back to Heather just as she let out a pained groan and closed her eyes. Tilting the glass toward her lips, he whispered, "Drink."

Her eyes remained shut, and her body lay still.

Watching, I had the strange impression that Father was trying to force a doll to drink.

"I am the Lord who heals you," he said, his voice force-ful but fraying at the edges. Then, more softly, "Exodus, 15:26."

"Your prayer isn't working," I said. "She needs a doc-tor."

"Get out!" he yelled. "The Lord is my shepherd! I shall not want! In your faithfulness and righteousness, come to my relief!"

"I'm going to get Doctor Johnson," I said. "I don't care what you say."

He stood and stabbed a finger toward me. "If you leave this house and go to Doctor Johnson, don't ever come back. If you put a man above God, you're not welcome here."

"If you put God above Heather," I shot back, jabbing a finger at my chest, "then you're not welcome *here*."

"Out!" he yelled.

"I'm getting Doctor Johnson!"

I ran down the hallway, flew down the stairs, flung open the door, leapt over the front steps, sprinted down the street to Dr. Johnson's house, where I pounded on the door with both fists until Mrs. Johnson opened it.

"Heather's dying!" I half-yelled, half-sobbed. "Doctor Johnson has to save her!"

A moment later, Dr. Johnson emerged with his medical bag in hand. We ran up the street to my house where I pushed open the garden gate and led him through the over-grown path and up the steps. I reached for the knob, twisted it and pushed, but the door wouldn't budge.

It was locked.

"I know another way in," I said breathlessly. "Wait here, I'll unlock it from inside."

I jumped off the steps and darted toward the alley.

"But why—?" Dr. Johnson said.

Before I could reach the alley, the front door swung open.

I stopped short and turned.

Dr. Johnson stood frozen, staring at the doorway.

Father stood there, both hands gripping his double-barrel shotgun, the muzzle pointed directly at Dr. Johnson's face.

"Off my property, Johnson," he growled, "or I'll blow your head off. I mean it."

Dr. Johnson's medical bag hit the ground. He turned and bolted toward the street.

Father turned the shotgun on me.

My gaze fell from his crimson, rage-filled face to his hands and the fingers wrapped tightly around the gun's twin triggers.

"Come in, boy, and I'll kill you," he said.

I stood frozen as he turned and went inside.

I was still standing there twenty minutes later when the door opened again. Father stood in the doorway, this time without the shotgun.

"She's gone," he said. "God took her."

"You'll be wanting some time alone, then?" Bridget said, her hand resting on the doorknob to my father's room.

"Yes."

"I'll be in the parlor."

I hesitated, my fingers brushing the amulet in my pocket. Healing and protection, I reminded myself. I drew a calming breath, then pushed the door open and stepped into the dimly lit room. It was smaller than I remembered.

So was the pale, emaciated figure in the bed.

I approached the man I'd spent most of my life trying to distance myself from. His eyes were closed. His chest barely rose and fell. As I watched him breathe, a single, rattling cough brought up a gob of blood-tinged sputum that clung to his lips. I took the rag from the bedside table and wiped it away.

I reached into my pocket and gripped the amulet. But after a moment's thought, I let it go. From the other pocket, I took a rosary. Its silver crucifix gleamed faintly in the candlelight. Our Lady of Prompt Succor gazed at me from her medallion.

I laid the crucifix on my father's chest and draped the beads across his hand. I picked up the Bible from the table and opened it to the first bookmarked page.

"The Lord is my shepherd," I read aloud. "I shall not want."

Father's breathing hitched.

"He maketh me to lie down in green pastures," I continued. "He leadeth me beside the still waters."

His hand shifted. His bony fingers curled around a few of the rosary beads.

I turned to the next marked passage. "The prayer of faith shall save the sick, and the Lord shall raise him up; and if he hath committed sins, they shall be forgiven him."

Father's other hand, trembling, lifted slowly and closed over the crucifix.

I turned to another page. "If you listen carefully to the Lord your God and do what is right in His eyes, if you pay attention to His commands and keep all His decrees, I will not bring on you any of the diseases I brought on the Egyptians, for I am the Lord who heals you. Exodus, 15:26."

His eyes opened, and he looked at me.

I rested my hand on his—the one gripping the crucifix —and recited a verse I'd once heard him read aloud, altering it now to fit the moment. "Heal him, O Lord, and I shall be healed. Save him, and I shall be saved."

"Hiram," he said, his voice weak, barely a whisper. "You came home."

I squeezed his hand. "I'm sorry I never visited. That I never answered your letters."

He shook his head slightly, then broke into a violent coughing fit. Specks of blood flecked my shirt.

"You did the best you could," I said, gripping his hand tighter. "You did what you thought was right."

He shook his head again.

"I'll go get Bridget," I said.

"No."

He withdrew his hand from mine and held out his frail, trembling arms. I leaned down and embraced him, careful not to hurt him.

"I'm sorry," he whispered. "For everything."

His arms fell away, limp against the bed.

"There's nothing to be sorry about," I said.

"Forgive me. Please."

"I do. I forgive you."

He nodded and closed his eyes.

That night, I slept soundly in my childhood bed.

Bridget woke me early in the morning to tell me my father had died.

35

We buried my father in Green-Wood Cemetery on a rare warm winter morning in Brooklyn. Bare branches stretching overhead cast pale, shifting shadows over the graves—his, my sister's, and my mother's. Birds sang merrily in the treetops.

Standing over my father's grave, Father Murphy said, "Do not let your hearts be troubled. You believe in God; believe also in me. My Father's house has many rooms." He went on to speak about my father's faith and his devotion to his family.

Bridget stood beside me, weeping quietly. "I was more than his caretaker, you know," she said through her tears.

I nodded.

"Life is full of pain and loss," Father Murphy said. "But also the hope of eternal life."

It made me smile. After all, what harm was there in hoping for something? *I should do more of that,* I thought.

Father Murphy sprinkled holy water on the casket and committed my father's soul to God. He glanced at us and nodded toward the shovel standing in the mound beside the grave. I stepped forward, took it, tossed the first shovelful onto the casket, and handed the shovel to Bridget, the sound of dirt striking wood still echoing in my ears.

"The Lord bless you and keep you," Father Murphy said. "The Lord make His face shine upon you and be gracious to you. The Lord turn His face toward you and give you peace."

When the service ended, Bridget turned to me, her face wet with tears, and we embraced. I told her I wanted a word with my mother and sister in private; I'd catch up with her shortly, as we planned to share the carriage back to the house.

Mother's grave lay just to the left of Father's, and Heather's was beside hers. I'd noticed the empty plot to the right of Father's and guessed he'd bought all four long ago. As much as I loved and missed my family and regretted not spending more time with Father, I didn't plan to join them here anytime soon. Nor did I believe I ever would. But who could say what the future held?

Standing at the foot of my sister's grave, I said, "Heather, I used to tell you Father let Mother die for no good reason, that it was the same as killing her with his own hands. I don't believe that anymore.

"You didn't deserve to die, but Father didn't kill you. God didn't kill you. Cholera killed you. People get sick, that's all. I don't know why. I wish I did. I went to medical college to look for the answer, to prove it didn't have to be that way. But I never found it, and I never proved anything."

I stepped over to Mother's grave.

"Mother, I can't believe there's a Heaven, even if I'd like to. I can't believe you're up there with Father, sitting together on God's knee." I looked up at the sky, at the drifting clouds, then back down at her grave. "I've believed a lot of things that turned out wrong. I hope this is one of them." I wiped away a tear. "You were a wonderful mother. Kind, loving, funny, beautiful. I don't know if you're in Heaven, or anywhere else. But I'll always know where to find you."

I rested my palm against my heart and choked back a sob.

36

Two days later, a letter arrived at my father's house, where I was staying while I settled affairs. It was from Nathaniel Kyper, my father's lawyer, inviting Bridget and me to meet with him at his office on Chambers Street the following Thursday to discuss the contents of Father's will.

"Have a seat," Kyper said, standing behind a walnut desk.

Bridget and I settled into the leather-upholstered chairs across from him.

"Cigar?" he offered, gesturing toward an ornate wooden box on the desk. I shook my head, mindful of Bridget's disapproval of tobacco. He selected one for himself, struck a match, and puffed until a cloud of smoke billowed above the desk. He sat down, leaned forward, and opened a file.

"Here we go," he said, glancing at us before reading aloud. "I, William G. Whitaker, of 307 MacDougal Street, being of sound mind and body, as witnessed here on this third day of November, 1850, hereby declare this to be my Last Will and Testament."

He adjusted his spectacles before continuing. "To my faithful servant, Bridget O'Malley, I leave the sum of fifteen hundred dollars."

"Oh, my God," Bridget said, her hand flying to her chest. "That's too much."

"Be that as it may, Miss O'Malley, that's what he left you." He took a bank draft from the file and slid it across the desk. "Don't spend it all in one place," he said with a wink.

She lifted it and read the sum, her lips moving silently. "Oh, God," she said. "Oh, heavens."

"All right," Kyper said. "Next item. My house, at 307 MacDougal Street, including all its contents at the time of my death..." He glanced at me before continuing. "I leave to Bridget O'Malley."

Bridget let out a yip, like a startled pup. The bank draft fluttered to the desktop. She looked up at the ceiling. "Thank you, William," she said, her voice trembling. And then she wept. "Oh God, I'm blubbering."

Once Bridget had composed herself and dabbed her eyes with a handkerchief, Kyper outlined the practical details pertaining to deeds, probate, and taxes. He noted that she could continue living at the house as long as she liked while everything was being settled. Afterward, she could do as she pleased with the property, which had recently been appraised for tax purposes at $11,500.

He closed the file. "That's all for now," he said.

Bridget put a hand on my arm. "You're welcome to stay while you sort out those New Orleans affairs," she said.

"Thank you, Bridget."

As she and I stood to leave, Kyper said, "Hiram, could you stick around for a moment? There are a few details I'd like to discuss."

"Of course," I replied.

After Bridget left, I settled back into the chair. Kyper re-opened the file and removed a sealed envelope, which he handed to me. "From your father," he said. "In the event you outlived him. I've kept it here for years. No need to read it right now. I'm sure it's personal." He took out three more sheets of paper and laid them on the desk between us. "I thought we should discuss these matters after Miss O'Malley left, as they don't pertain to her."

I nodded.

He held up the top sheet. "Last Will and Testament," he read, "William G. Whitaker, Addendum, June 4, 1852. If, at the time of my death, Bridget O'Malley is still alive, and my son, Hiram T. Whitaker, has predeceased me, I leave the following to Bridget O'Malley. If my son has not passed, I leave the following to him. One: the townhouse at 103 Orchard Street."

103 Orchard Street?

"My father's house is at 307 MacDougal Street."

Kyper chuckled and puffed on his cigar. "Not the same house, son."

I stared at the sheet of paper, trying to grasp his meaning. "He had another house?"

"He did. He's leased it to tenants since before you were born. I've been managing it for him since he purchased it. I doubt Miss O'Malley knows anything about it."

He leaned back and studied his cigar while I tried to absorb this new information.

"I can't believe it," I said.

"Nonetheless, it's true."

"Could I have that cigar, then?"

He reached into the box, handed me one, and struck a match. I leaned forward as he held the flame to the cigar's tip. I took a slow draw, sat back, and watched the smoke curl upward as I tried to grasp the implications of this news.

"Now, where was I?" Kyper said. He ran his finger down the page. "Ah, yes. Two: The tenement building at 54 Bleecker Street."

That was where Emma lived.

"What about it?" I said.

"It's yours now."

That same evening, I went to Emma's and invited her to dinner at Delmonico's. I told her my father had left me a little money—and, more importantly, that we'd reconciled at the end—and I wanted to celebrate by treating her to a fancy dinner.

She threw her arms around me. "Oh my God, yes."

Our table, by the window overlooking Beaver Street, was one of the better ones, set with silver, crystal, and a single candle in a gleaming silver holder. As we caught up over oysters and turtle soup, Emma asked me about my plans. She was tactful, careful not to ask whether I'd inherited enough to settle the Chartres Street matter. She did, however, express surprise that my father had left the house to Bridget instead of me.

"She deserved it," I said. "She was there for him when no one else was."

"You'll stay in New York, though, won't you? Even if you don't want to be a doctor—at least for now? New York is so wonderful, and New Orleans is so… terrifying."

I nodded. "I don't really know what my plans are yet."

She set down her glass of champagne and took my hand.

"I like you very much, Hiram. I would miss you terribly if you left."

"I like you, too," I replied.

"Do you like me very much?"

"Yes. Very much."

Her face lit up, just as a violinist in the corner struck the opening notes of *Jeanie with the Light Brown Hair.*

"My song!" Emma exclaimed. "I think this is one of the happiest nights of my life."

Later, as we shared a Baked Alaska, she said, almost as an afterthought, "Would you like to come by my apartment tonight? You must barely fit into that little bed of yours at your father's house."

I set my fork down and wiped my mouth with a linen napkin.

"It's a tempting invitation," I said. "But I'm not quite up to it yet. This whole thing with my father has left me feeling… drained."

She glanced down at the last bite of Baked Alaska. "I understand. It must feel terrible, losing your last remaining family. I'm sorry, Hiram. It was presumptuous of me."

I reached across the table and placed my hand on hers.

"It wasn't presumptuous, Emma. I just need a little more time."

* * *

The following Monday, I joined Mr. Kyper at his office for a meeting with Patience and Sarah Dufilho and their attorneys. After much discussion, we reached an agreement: I would sell the Orchard Street townhouse, appraised at $15,500, and use some of the proceeds to buy out Sarah Dufilho and her children's fifty percent share of the Chartres Street house, valued at $18,500. I would use the rental income from the Bleecker Street building to pay Patience the outstanding rent on the Chartres Street house and buy out her half over the next five years.

After all the documents were signed and the others had departed, I remained behind to speak with Kyper. We arranged for Emma's rent at 54 Bleecker Street to be waived entirely, beginning the first of the following month, for as long as she wished to live there.

A few evenings later, I went to see her.

She peeked out, then swung the door open and jumped into my arms.

"I've missed you," she said. "I'm still thinking about you and our incredible dinner together. I can still taste that heavenly roast duck."

I held her close.

"I'm going back to New Orleans," I said.

Instead of letting me go, she held me tighter.

"I know," she whispered.

I stayed at Bridget O'Malley's house for several more weeks and spent Christmas Eve with Emma at her parents' home in Brooklyn. Bridget had begun seeing someone new and spent the holiday with him and his children in Harlem. I spent Christmas Day wandering the snowy streets alone.

On New Year's Day, I boarded a train bound for Philadelphia.

37

I sat with Mary Beth's parents in their front room and recounted everything that had happened since I last saw them. I explained how I'd written to the telegraph office in Saint Louis, which had relayed my messages to Fort Laramie. Through these exchanges, I'd contacted the fort's commander, who put me in touch with a stonemason in the nearby town of the same name. I arranged for a tombstone to be placed at the head of Mary Beth's grave, which they had found using my directions. I also arranged for a minister to deliver a proper Christian eulogy when the stone was placed.

"I would have liked to have been there," I said. "But the next wagon train won't leave until June, and there are things I have to take care of in New Orleans."

"We understand," Mr. Johansson said.

"You can't imagine how much this means to us," Mrs. Johansson said.

I took a folded sheet of paper from my coat pocket and handed it to Mr. Johansson. "I hope this is all right."

He read it aloud:

Mary Beth WHITAKER
née Johansson

May 29, 1832 – June 8, 1852

Beloved Daughter and Wife
Her light shone briefly but brightly

"The Lord is my shepherd; I shall not want."
Psalm 23:1

Forever in our hearts.

After a long moment, Mr. Johansson folded the paper and placed it carefully on the table.

"That's perfect, son. Thank you."

38

I had returned to New Orleans a few days earlier to find the ground floor of Whitaker's Apothecary & Healing Arts transformed into a shop selling potions, dolls, gris-gris bags, and an assortment of other voodoo paraphernalia. Upstairs, Jerome had converted the second floor into a stylish hair salon called Jerome's.

"We knew you'd be back someday," he said. "We just didn't know when. We hoped you wouldn't mind."

"Not at all," I replied.

Now, on a crisp, sunny February morning, the three of us sat on my third-floor balcony, drinking Jerome's strong coffee. I'd told them everything that had happened up north. Though I couldn't yet afford to pay Charlotte her twenty-five percent of the house, I had arranged for new documents to formalize her one-quarter share.

"You know I didn't forge anything, right?" Charlotte said. "You believe me."

"I believe you."

"Good. Then you won't mind if I call this place Whitaker's Voodoo Supply," she said.

The three of us burst out laughing.

"You think I'm kidding? I'm serious."

"I think it's perfect," I said.

"Either that or Charlotte France Herbal Remedies."

"That's a good one, too."

"So if you're not going back to doctoring," Jerome said, "what are you going to do with your life?"

"I've been thinking about trying my hand at art. I used to scribble a bit."

"Art? You mean drawings and such?"

"That's right. And I've been thinking about writing something, too."

"Writing?" they said together, incredulous.

I nodded. "I thought I might write a novel."

"What about?" Charlotte asked.

"A Northerner who comes down to New Orleans and falls under the spell of some local voodoo practitioners who use him for their own purposes. Or something like that. I haven't really given it much thought."

"That sounds ridiculous," Charlotte said. "Can I read it when you're done?"

Epilogue

I woke to the rhythmic sound of water lapping against the ship's hull. I had fallen asleep on the deck the night before, watching for shooting stars, and dreamt of Wyoming. Now the sky above, scattered with clouds, so closely resembled the Wyoming sky that, for a moment, I wondered whether I was still there, lying beside our wagon, dying perhaps, or stretched out in the grave Baron Sunday had dug for me.

I knew White Wolf and Cold Moon had been killed months earlier in a cavalry massacre, but part of me still expected them to appear, blocking the sky as they reached down to save me and Mary Beth.

Instead, it was Jerome who appeared.

"I'm making breakfast," he said.

I could smell the coffee.

I stood and scanned the horizon. We'd been at sea for several weeks and should reach Rio de Janeiro within a day or two to replenish our supplies. But for now, there was no land in sight—only the beautiful, infinite blue stretching out in all directions.

"Give me a moment," I said.

Jerome headed back to the ship's galley.

Was this all preordained? I wondered. This moment, and everything that had happened during the past two years?

From the moment I was born? Or from the day Heather died?

I didn't know. I would never know. Just as I would never ask certain questions of Jerome or Charlotte.

I turned from the rail and made my way to the galley, where I took a seat beside a few members of the pirate crew.

"I tried your Coca-Kola," said a tall, older crew member with a long gray beard we'd taken to calling Graybeard. "I think you're onto something. You're gonna sell a ton of that stuff in California."

Jerome turned from the stove and began piling steaming hotcakes onto our plates just as Charlotte walked in. She kissed me on the top of the head and sat down beside me, resting a hand on my leg.

"Good morning, beautiful people," she said.

"Mornin', gorgeous," Graybeard replied.

Just then, Napoleon leapt onto the table, sniffed my hotcakes, lay down, and curled into a ball in a warm patch of sunlight shining through the hatch above. He began to purr.

"That cat's one hell of a mouser," Graybeard said.

"He sure is," I agreed.

The End

Hiram Truth Whitaker —
San Francisco, CA — August 11, 1855

ACKNOWLEDGMENTS

I would like to thank Marsha Elleston, Jerome Sopoçko, Kelly Dixon, Susan Townsend, Dona Haber, Laura Wyles, and Ed Lee for their sharp eyes and helpful suggestions. My gratitude to Mark Thomas, whose cover painting beautifully captures the spirit of the Chartres Street townhouse; and to Owen Ever, for walking me through the landscape—both real and imagined—that inspired this story.

ABOUT THE AUTHOR

Blake Haber is a cigar roller living in Santa Barbara, California.
Hiram's Faith is his first novel.